Bom Boy

By Yewande Omotoso

CATALYST PRESS
Livermore, California

For further information, write Catalyst Press,
2941 Kelly Street, Livermore CA 94551
or email info@catalystpress.org

Originally published under the title

Bom Boy

by Modjaji Books (South Africa)

FIRST EDITION

10 9 8 7 6 5 4 3 2 1

Library of Congress Control Number: 2018946322

Cover design by Karen Vermeulen, Cape Town, South Africa

Printed in Canada

To my Mother

FRIDAY 13TH JULY 2001

A thing began to grow like a tree in Lékè's throat. It was the same thing that grew when he was picked for the school play and it was there when he was later cut from the cast. It was there when girls glanced away as he walked down the corridors. An invisible rash.

As the day approached, Lékè dreaded turning nine. Jane had mentioned to him that they would have a party to celebrate—this was something that had never happened before.

"Why?" He was helping her in the kitchen.

"It's a special one," she said, dusting flour off his nose. "Last of the single digits. Next is ten—two numbers instead of one."

Lékè was certain that having his own party was a bad idea, but this certainty only existed during the day. At school, he moved from class to class, a watery feeling; his hearing dulled as if his head were submerged in liquid. He could barely hear what people said, couldn't talk back, how was he to host a party?

In his dreams, at night, though, there was no question. He stood surrounded by a crowd of boys; they were laughing and patting him on the back. They played on the school cricket grounds and Lékè hit a century, running the pitch he'd tripped on during the day to a chorus of sniggers.

"Cardboard boy." That was what the other kids called him because of the strange crackers Jane packed in his lunchbox. Or "kid-for-hire" because one of the older boys had seen Jane and Marcus at the parents' evening and worked out that Lékè was adopted.

Along with the threat of a party, the other thing that changed with the coming of his birthday was Marcus.

Lékè walked towards the familiar red car but was surprised to find a balding head and heavy brown leather jacket in place of Jane's blonde hair peeping from underneath a scarf.

"Hey." Marcus leaned across to unlock the passenger door.

Lékè settled himself.

"Good day? How was practice?"

Someone had tripped him, he'd got grass in his mouth. "Fine."

Marcus pulled off the verge. "Going past the rope shop, all-right?" He looked over at Lékè. "Taking you sailing this weekend. Early gift." He was jovial in a way Lékè was unaccustomed to.

At a red traffic light, Marcus reached his arm across and ruffled Lékè's afro.

"Where'll we go?"

"Well..." The light changed and the car eased forward. "We'll leave from the Waterfront, just go round the bay— it's great, you'll love it."

◆◆

"Does he even want to sail?" Jane spat into the sink. She rinsed her toothbrush and placed it in the porcelain holder, studying herself briefly. Lékè would be nine and she'd be forty-nine.

"He seems OK about it," Marcus answered.

"And the whole cricket thing?" Jane entered the room, her hands smoothed over her hair that was now growing back.

"Yes. Look," Marcus said when he saw Jane's expression. "It's time he came out more, that's all I'm trying to do here. Always shuffling around...playing by himself." Marcus removed his robe and climbed into bed. He reached towards the pile of books and papers balanced on his side table and switched on the lamp.

Jane sat on the edge of her side of the bed and pulled on a pair of socks. She didn't like Marcus's tone but she was also distracted. She walked to the vanity. Her regular ritual of putting on face cream had ended months before, but tonight, maybe it was the growing hair, she enjoyed the cool paste against her skin and the glow it left on her cheekbones. Can stop with the scarves now, she thought.

She touched her hair again. Yes, just long enough to stop the scarves. She smoothed balm over her lips and the mint brought her back to the room, to her husband. She turned to address him. "I don't think you should force him. Not unless he looks like he's actually having fun."

"Fun?" Marcus scowled. "That's a long way away, dear. I'm just trying to get the boy to act normal." Jane shook her head and Marcus raced to defend himself. "I don't mean it like that, you know what I mean."

Jane sighed. She studied him, noticing a slight paunch where he leaned over the book in his lap which, ignoring her gaze, he now opened and pretended to read. Greying temples. His bald pate, sun-bleached and liver-spotted.

"Marcus."

"Hmmm?" He looked up.

"The cricket team, for instance. He told me he doesn't want to play any more. Coach seemed amenable."

"Well, I spoke to the coach. It's good for him, Jane. He'll get used to it. Can you trust me on this one? He's a nine-year-old boy, he needs to run around and hit things."

She still felt so tired, not always up for combat. She settled on her back, trying to think of a response. Marcus took silence for dissent. He leaned across and kissed her on the cheek.

"Don't worry so much. He'll be OK."

They held eyes for a few seconds. Marcus put his hand to the side of her face and Jane remembered strong arms; that was the first thing she'd noticed about him twenty years ago when they'd met. And his fingers, beautiful and lean.

While courting, he'd sent her pencil sketches—his favorite fossils, 500 million years old. She'd written him poetry. A progression of affairs until she'd finally written:

Let's grow old together.
The way green leaves turn brown together
and fall from trees.
Let's grow old together.
The way blossoms curl up and their colors softly stir:

Let's grow old and die together.

Marcus returned to his book, reading for real this time. Jane looked at him some more and eventually he turned. "You OK?"

She shook it off. "Nothing."

Marcus smoothed a defiant tuft of her hair and smiled. He put away his book and switched off the light, coaxing her head onto his chest.

Jane slept light. This was her custom even before the treatment. The slightest disturbance startled her. When they were married and first sharing a bed, Marcus teased her about it. Over the years, it had at times become a source of quiet strain between them. As a boy, Lékè was not one to sleep through the night. It became a habit of his to clamber into their bed around midnight and stay there till morning. "We shouldn't allow this," Marcus often chastised her the following day, but she could see that even he couldn't say no to the boy when he appeared, frightened, at the foot of their bed the following night. In any case, this continued for many years and had only just stopped recently. Jane wondered if Marcus's renewed vigor in insisting Lékè hit a ball and throw things was inspired by this development.

Perhaps Marcus took his cue from Lékè after all. Because no one had asked him to stop, one night he'd simply not shown up. "All right?" Jane had asked the next morning at breakfast. Lékè had nodded and that was that.

She would never confess it to Marcus, he would roll his eyes, but Jane missed Lékè, she missed the shape of him at 1 am beside her, warm and damp with sweat; she missed the sound of his labored breath—he was not asthmatic but wheezed nonetheless; the violence of his deep sleep in contrast to her still shallow one, he'd start off parallel to her and Marcus, lying between them, but somehow end up perpendicular, his limbs flailed out in the night from the force of whatever dreams he dreamed. She missed him with something much firmer than just a sense of her boy growing up. She felt he wasn't so much growing up as disappearing. Or perhaps it was she who was disappearing. Of course that was all she could think after the doctor gave his final diagnosis. My boy. What will happen to my boy? Despite a great recovery, responding to the medications, the weight of it still pressed on her each day. She wished she could transfer the heaviness of that onto Marcus's chest so he could understand the proper nature of the responsibility they bore.

As if aware he was in her thoughts, Marcus began to snore and Jane slipped into her dreamless sleep.

❦

Despite Jane's attempts to dissuade him, Marcus persisted with the sailing mission. It was important even if Jane didn't seem to understand that. You can't coddle forever, soon enough the boy must go out, must puff his chest. Marcus finished arranging the display of sailing knots on the dining table and shouted for Lékè to join him. The boy was outside digging with Jane in the garden. Enough with the flowers.

"Lékè, come here!"

Lékè entered from the garden, his knees caked in soil.

Marcus felt his own excitement double even in the face of Lékè's clear lack of enthusiasm. "Look at all this! Ready?"

Lékè nodded, approached the table sullen.

"OK, good." Marcus understood he was not to give in. He so often just wished to shake the boy, shake him out of whatever he was stuck in. It was a real impulse but Marcus restrained himself. He is just a boy, he heard Jane's voice in his head. And it was true, he was just a boy. So for now he would resort to teaching Lékè how to tie sailing knots. "Now which do you want to learn first?"

Lékè scanned the table. Marcus had taken care to cover it with old newspaper before laying out the knotted ropes. A friend from the sailing school had loaned them to him, four ties in total. Two were white and wound around grey metal bars, the other two were green and red—Lékè pointed to these.

"Very good. Sheet bend and reef knot. Let's start with reef." Marcus collected Lékè into his arms and settled on a chair. "Aah! Big boy!"

Lékè shifted. He often preferred not to be touched.

"Ready?" Marcus was struggling to balance Lékè and disassemble the knot. It would be easier to let Lékè simply stand and watch but having gone this route, holding the boy against his chest, he thought it best not to retreat. He could feel his operation delicate, risking collapse at any moment.

Lékè's limbs, long for his age, straddled his father's lap and his tennis shoes scraped the floor. With his arms around Lékè, Marcus finally released the knot.

"This one," Marcus said. "Reef knot...or square knot is very easy. You do it every day, my boy, your laces." Marcus pumped his thigh to emphasize his point and Lékè's shoes made scuffing noises on the floor. Marcus began to tie the knot again. "You watching?"

Lékè nodded. Indeed, for a few seconds he was watching, then Marcus noticed the shift of attention as the boy put his hands to his throat.

"What's that?" Marcus asked, feeling he already knew the answer.

"My throat."

For a few weeks now, Lékè had been complaining of something in his throat. He complained to Jane perhaps because, Marcus thought, Lékè didn't expect sympathy from his father.

"What's wrong with your throat?" Marcus asked, defeat already in his voice.

"It's tight. Scratching."

"Yes, but what exactly?" Marcus challenged, but as always Jane was right there, when had she entered the house?

"You okay, Lékè?"

"He says his throat is scratching." Marcus tried to wipe the incredulity from his voice. His wife had explained that it wasn't a figment of the boy's imagination as Marcus had accused, he was actually allergic to something, they just had to figure out what. Allergic to knots. And ball throws.

And me, thought Marcus.

"Come, sweetheart," said Jane and Lékè was rescued from the afternoon's lesson.

◆◆

Lékè stuffed the Spiderman invitations into his locker and left them there.

"Should I call the mothers?" Jane wondered out loud at dinner when no responses had come and the birthday was three days away.

Lékè sat at one end of the table, Marcus on the other and Jane along the length. Lékè played with the lettuce Jane had harvested from her vegetable patch, stabbing it with his fork. Marcus studied the boy, then he said, "I think it's fine, Jane."

"What do you mean, it's fine?"

"Maybe let just us celebrate."

Jane seemed to be considering this.

"Besides, I don't really feel like a hoard of marauding kids stampeding through the house. Lightness is away— we'd have to do the clean-up ourselves."

Jane stared long first at Marcus and then at Lékè, both suddenly inscrutable. After another few minutes, Marcus leaned over and squeezed Jane's shoulder. "Let's do that then. Just us." He winked at Lékè who looked back down at his plate, stabbed the lettuce leaf one final time, and shoved it into his mouth.

The last of the single digits, Lékè's ninth birthday passed quiet as a ghost.

In the end, there was no sailing. Lékè wouldn't learn the knots and Marcus gave up. Their small victory of dissuading Jane from throwing a party no one would come to anyway receded and a familiar distance took up between father and son. Even Jane struggled to guess at what Lékè would want as a gift so they forsook the element of surprise for certainty and asked him. An atlas, he said, and a globe to place in his bedroom.

Even if Lékè would never sail, it didn't mean, in his dreams, that he did not travel.

That year, during the September holidays, Lékè spent the Spring days either in the garden with Jane or, when it rained, he laid on the cool wooden floor of his room, his arm propping up his head as he scoured the large atlas. His parents were happy to see him preoccupied with something they could understand. Even Jane, often so quick to defend Lékè against Marcus, agreed that it was good, his sudden interest in geography, in maps and adventure. They let him be. The days mushed together like pages of a forgotten book, sodden and alone.

Back at school, Lékè struggled through. Marcus's attempts to toughen him, straighten him up, had not been unfruitful. Lékè listened harder and he made an attempt to raise his voice and be heard.

At the end of each day, to stumble into his dreams—into a terrain he was adept at navigating—was a relief. The confusions of the day slipped off his skin like sweat.

His dreams were often more real than "real life." Lékè cherished the characters he encountered—some recognizable from the daytime, some not—as well as the surge of joy and life that powered his sleep. The wind blew different here, softer.

A year later, when Lékè turned ten, he owned a library of atlases and a collection of globes that ranged from a key-ring to a basketball-sized sphere. Jane had fallen ill again and her garden threatened to overrun itself in her absence. She'd asked Lékè to care for it while she got her strength back and offered to pay him a stipend.

"Then you'll take it seriously," she'd said.

Lékè earned enough money gardening to tag along when Marcus did the grocery shopping, and visit the second-hand bookshop opposite the Spar to buy more atlases.

"Don't you have enough of those, Lékè?"

"No."

They drove back home in silence. With Jane ill, either in bed or in the hospital, the house had begun to change.

"Set the table. I'll go collect Mum," Marcus said,

dropping Lékè off.

They never answered his questions when he asked, and Lékè was not allowed to come along to the hospital.

"What's wrong with her?" he tried to ask now, again.

"Don't be difficult, Lékè. She's not feeling well, that's all. Come on, we'll be back soon. Use this key. Remember to lock the door behind you."

Lékè thought he'd watch the car pull off but Marcus kept the engine idling as he waited to see Lékè safely in the house. His head hung down, Lékè entered the house and locked the door behind him. He began to lay the table.

Jane had been away for a week this time and when they'd spoken on the phone two nights before, she'd sounded far away, further than she'd ever been. Something made Lékè think of Christmas and birthdays, happier times. There was a special cream-colored table cloth Jane liked to use: "hand-crocheted," she always said with pride. She'd bought it at a farm stall on one of their forages through the countryside looking for flower shows. And there were her favorite place mats—fat white ducks waddling across a red background. Remembering where she kept them, Lékè entered his parents' bedroom and, watching his footing, climbed up the cupboard till he could reach the top section.

His left foot was on a lower shelf and his right was bent and higher. He balanced himself by holding onto one of the shelves above and, with his right hand, reaching over his head at the top-top section. He heard the tap of his hand as he searched for the soft fabric. His hand connected and he tugged at a corner and let the cloth fall to the ground.

Next—the box with the mats. He reached a bit deeper, straining, and almost lost his balance. His shoulder was sore. He reached again and felt something round. Not it. Tired, he stepped his way back to the ground and collected the table cloth. At least that would make her smile, he thought, but then something on the floor caught his eye. It was an old photograph, sepia-colored and stained at the back so Lékè couldn't read what was written there. He wiped the dust off. A name, maybe. He turned it around and saw the face of a woman he didn't know. He kept the photo, thinking that he would ask Jane when they were next gardening, just the two of them. He heard the slam of a car door and ran out to spread the table cloth.

SATURDAY 25TH JULY 1992

Oscar took up the pen and started writing.

Dear Lékè,

I was five when I first heard my father sing:

Babaláwo mo wá bẹ̀bẹ̀

Alugbinrin

Ògùngùn tó ṣe fún mi lẹ́rẹ̀ kàn

Alugbinrin

Óní nma má fọwọ̀ kẹnu

Alugbinrin

Óní nma má fẹsẹ̀ kẹnu

Alugbinrin

Gbòngbò lo yè mí gẹ̀rẹ̀

Alugbinrin

Mo fọwọ́ kan ọbẹ̀ mó fí kẹnu

Alugbinrin

Mo bojú wo kùn ó rí gbendu

Alugbinrin

Babaláwo mo wá bẹ̀bẹ̀

◄◄►►

"Don't scare him with your stories," my mother said.

I can hear my father singing, feel the vibration of his deep voice. His singing always makes me think of soil. I don't know if that's because of his heavy earthy voice or because invariably when there was singing, we were on the farm. I remember the soil, moist and almost black.

"Bom Boy!" my father would shout in celebration once we'd finished making the yam heaps. Once I heard that, I knew a story was coming.

WEDNESDAY 19TH FEBRUARY 1992

Oscar walked up through the brush towards Rhodes Memorial. The higher he went through the forest, the leaves sieved the noise from his head, the tangle of thoughts caught in the branches above the Silverleaf Tree. Elaine had phoned him on the cellphone but he'd ignored her. If he spoke to her now he was worried she would hear it in his voice, hear what he was thinking and planning. With the baby coming, there was no need to add to her anxiety.

It had been easy to get the physical address for Malcolm Feathers. You would think someone with such a past would be hiding but there the address was, in the phone book like every other normal person. Even though Oscar had pressed her, Elaine would not be specific about what her guardian, Malcolm Feathers, had done to her all those years ago. But Oscar understood, from her visible scars and from the invisible ones, that the man had done the opposite of what that title prescribes. Guardian. Not only the opposite but the extreme worst. One night when Oscar had reached for Elaine in the bed they shared and she'd shuddered, he'd asked her outright. He knew he shouldn't, that she would tell him if and when she chose to, but he couldn't help himself. Did he touch you, Oscar had asked. She'd turned away, then crawled out of the bed, then gathered her things. She'd disappeared for a week then returned with a small smile and he'd understood that he was never to ask again.

Oscar dug his hands into his pockets; his long legs took wide strides, the exertion and the crunch of the ground a welcome distraction from what lay ahead.

It was the middle of February and each day the Cape Town sun poured itself out. Later, simmering, it lay down in nights that were dark but not cool. The air was palpable as students stumbled back onto the campus: in a stupor from the heat, alcohol, or the shock of work after long holidays—Oscar couldn't tell.

He checked his watch, just after seven. He'd continue walking for another few minutes before setting out. The plan was to go by the house, the Feathers' residence. Just drive by. Maybe, if he saw a light on, maybe knock on the door. It was all a muddle in Oscar's head but the compulsion to act on the muddle was strong, as if a drug was in his veins, telling him left was right, up was down and so on. He was going to be a father. He wanted to knock on the monster's door and then what? What happened in the fairytales? Vanquish the monster so his wife would sleep at night, so his wife would not first shudder when he reached for her. So his son would grow up strong and happy. So they could all be happy. Look the monster in the eye. Vanquish him.

Oscar found a path through the bush and, at the top of his climb, came out into the parking lot. He noticed a short plump girl with freckled cheeks. She walked with a skinny boy and they carried a picnic basket between them, the handles at different heights, askew, the straw squeaking as they lumbered back down towards the campus.

It was still light out and there was a scattering of tourists climbing up the giant granite steps of the monument. Along either side of the steps, four life-size bronze lions, blue-green from a century of oxidation, sat on their haunches. A little girl and a man stood by one of the granite plinths and with some difficulty, the man hoisted the girl onto the lion's back. A woman a few steps down took a picture.

Oscar walked up the steps; grudgingly, he took in the palm-to-cheek bust of Cecil John Rhodes arranged on the top platform amidst imposing Doric columns. At the top, Oscar turned to enjoy the view: the stone terrace at the bottom of the monument; the curved stone wall; the forests with an army of towering spindly trees leaning away from the Southeaster; and the familiar shapes and lines of the surrounding neighborhoods.

Visiting the monument had become a ritual of Oscar's since he'd arrived in Cape Town, over a year ago, to take up a post at the University. South Africa had been lonelier than he'd anticipated, perhaps, Oscar mused, its population caught up in their transition and all the energy this required. He found his colleagues hostile at best, insulting of his academic fitness at worst. Soon after he arrived, Oscar began taking strolls through the campus but even this was insufficient to walk off the loneliness, the sense of umbrage; soon enough, he started climbing through the brambles that edged Ring Road. Sometimes he found a path, many times he was happy to bundhu bash, not caring if the forest dragged at his trousers or scraped his moccasins. He liked to come up on Ol' CJ, as he thought of him in his mind. Liked to discover him the way Vasco da Gama had discovered things, the way David Livingstone did. Oscar had even made a joke about it back at the department. "I discovered this humongous statue up there," he said. Many colleagues lacked the sense of humor required. Some got it and smiled weakly. Most ignored him.

Strangely, Oscar had continued to seek out the Rhodes statue in a bid to feel close to home. Not for the reason that the statue reminded him of anything back home but rather for the exact opposite. The giant shrine to Rhodes contrasted with the simple life-size statue of the revered Mọ́rẹ̀mí behind Ōdùdūwà Hall back on Ile-Ife campus in Nigeria. Oscar remembered visiting the small courtyard as a little boy: a series of chalky statues memorializing Yoruba history. His favorite was Mọ́rẹ̀mí: head bent, hands clasped together and resting on her raised thigh; the intricate detail of her braided hair. His father would lift him up so he could study the sculpted plaits.

"That's the hairstyle of queens."

"Why?"

"Because you see how all the hair catches up in the center like that? Sùkú. Only women who don't need to carry produce to the market can afford to plait their hair that way. Queens."

"Was Mọ́rẹ̀mí a queen?"

"Not in the beginning. But she made a sacrifice and became one."

"How?"

Relishing the memory, Oscar walked down, back through the sloped forest and to where he'd parked his car on Ring Road.

Mọ́rẹ̀mí's story had dotted his childhood with the consistency of birthdays. Oscar was surprised on arriving at the University of Cape Town to find that some of the people he shared a lab with had never heard of Mọ́rẹ̀mí. Those that bothered to apologize claimed their field of science was responsible and they promised to read more but Oscar found the excuses thin. Many of his colleagues didn't even know in which segment of the continent to look in order to find Nigeria on a map.

"I thought you were colored," one said, confused by Oscar's clay-brown skin and curly hair.

This in fact was a preferable address to the person that had simply approached him one day and asked: What are you?

Oscar had inherited little of his father's dark complexion and his light brown hair and oyinbo mother had made him an easy target for teasing in primary school in Nigeria.

The ignorance of his university colleagues mixed with the opulence of Rhodes Memorial had brewed distaste in Oscar. Here in this country, he realized, they memorialized wealthy white men—thieves; back home in Nigeria, simple people who sacrificed for the group.

Many a late evening at the Rugby Club, Oscar had found himself defending a country that faced easy derision among his South African colleagues. Here, not just among his lab partners, historians and political scientists weighed in. Decades from independence, Nigeria was an inert giant, burdened by greed. Against more informed opponents, Oscar had needed every detail he could find to play the game of one-upmanship. The more beer consumed, the more animated and irrational the conversation.

"For instance, your Rhodes," Oscar said, finishing a Castle and hailing for another.

A few men laughed because an icon of their past had been, in a sentence, bequeathed to them like a trinket.

"Our Rhodes."

"Yes! Your Rhodes. If Mọ́rẹ̀mí got into a fight with that man, ah—she'd finish him off. Easy!"

This deep in the night, this far into drinking, such fanciful arguments were seized upon with an earnestness the professors, while sober, reserved for the task of guiding their students.

"She'll probably use poison," a small voice said.

"No!" Oscar took offense to a hidden insult. "I'm not talking poison. Hand-to-hand combat."

"Thing is," a large man with a plump British accent began. His voice commanded a certain respect which Oscar resented—the man was an idiot. "Thing is, there would be no fight. Mọ́rẹ̀mí or what have you would simply be part of a mass of people—"

"Black people!"

"A mass of people building whatever Rhodes, or any other of the pioneers for that matter, had the foresight to envisage."

"Nonsense!" Oscar fought alone most nights.

Regardless of all the noise about "transformation," the University was pale and male and, he supposed, whatever color and estrogen there was, they didn't frequent the Rugby Club. He went out of loneliness, it's true, but also for this, to shake a fist at the fools and to let them know that he was still here, still standing. "You call that foresight? I call it theft."

Sometimes the evenings maintained a strained joviality, but often they ended in blatant tension. If his colleagues had listened, Oscar would have told them, the way his father had told him, the story of Mọ́rẹ̀mí who, leaving her only son and husband, offered herself as a prisoner when Ile-Ife was being invaded by neighboring warriors.

"What are warriors?" he'd asked his dad.

"Fighters. Soldiers. Now listen and don't interrupt me."

Six years old, Oscar settled back into bed. He noticed how the springs bent towards his father's weight. He closed his eyes.

"Once Mọ́rẹ̀mí was captured, the King noticed how beautiful she was and married her. She joined his house and also became part of the town. She learned all their secrets."

"What secrets, Daddy?"

"The things they were hiding. Now listen, as soon as she found out how to defeat them, she ran away from the palace and returned to Ife."

"Where did she come to? Did she come here, to Road 7? Or did she come to Staff School hall? Or...or..."

"Shhh. Don't interrupt! She returned to Ife. Back then there was no Road 7 or Staff or anything. She told the Ife army the secret and soon the Ūgbòs were defeated. Mórēmí then went to Esinmirin—"

"What is that?"

"E-sin-mi-rin. The goddess of the river. Mórēmí went to her to make a sacrifice of thanks. An offering. She gave fowls and bullocks and sheep, but the goddess demanded her only son."

Oscar sat up in bed. He felt in fact that he was that boy, felt his life suddenly precarious.

"What happened, Daddy?"

"Mórēmí could not refuse. She threw her son into the raging river."

His father always took long pauses as he neared the end of his stories.

"To comfort her, make her feel better, all the children of Ife took Mórēmí as a mother. So you see, Oscar, you have two mothers, always remember that." He patted the blanket, a sign that he was about to get up and switch the lights off.

"Does that mean I got born two times?"

His father just smiled.

Parents never answered the important questions.

The February sun finally dipped, a translucent orange peel coiled through the stone pines, the Silverleaf, and the rugged fynbos. Oscar checked his watch again.

FRIDAY 20TH JULY 2012

The Western Medical Fund office often felt too vast, too full of people and noise for Lékè but the job was easy and it meant that, each weekday, he knew where to come. He'd grown used to it in the time he'd been there. It had taken his colleagues a bit longer to acclimatize to him. Very

soon, once he started working at Western, Lékè's choice of
clothing became a topic for secret discussion. On prepar-
ing for his first job, it had seemed proper to Lékè to pick
one outfit and recycle it weekly. A pair of dark grey trousers
and a white short-sleeve shirt. Midweek he swapped the
white shirt for a light blue one. On Saturdays he went to
the laundromat. Someone complained. Lékè was said to be
unhygienic. A thin bone-white woman said that he smelled.
The manager pulled Lékè aside. A short awkward conversation was had, the result of which was a trip to Woolworths.
Lékè bought a black pair of trousers and a third collared
shirt, white with navy-blue stripes. Simultaneously, as if
roused by the gossip, the HR Department circulated a flyer
on the company dress code. A month on, they launched
a series of voluntary workshops with the conspicuous title
"Tolerance in the Workplace."

Things seemed to settle at Western. There was still
much for his colleagues to balk at but like all things, his
presence grew familiar even while it remained peculiar.
Time continued and, for the most part, Lékè was left alone.

The walk from the Western Medical Fund office to Lékè's
home was thirty minutes. Only on Fridays, Lékè veered from
his normal route.

He watched the pavement as he walked, and his long
legs swung a slow easy gait. He felt like whistling but he'd
never picked it up as a child, and now, nearing twenty, he
was too embarrassed to try. When he was around others
who whistled, he studied them, hoping to catch on to the
secret. Alone again, he would try it but to no avail.

As Lékè had entered manhood, Marcus found himself
unable to force him to visit the barber shop. The curly afro
was left to grow, twisting bronze-colored strands standing
out from his head like crooked wires. His hair was the color
of his eyes and his skin, the effect striking enough such
that, for a short period when he first arrived in high school,
Lékè was awarded the nickname Brownie. By the time he
entered Technikon and enrolled in Computer Science, Lékè
had shrugged off the nickname but not the silence that was

read as weakness in high school and arrogance at Tech. When he graduated, Lékè knew all about Programming; he'd learned the quiet language of computers and was satisfied to do that for a living. He had also, by then, learned to speak loud enough to be heard. He'd transitioned like an amphibian into an uncomfortable adulthood. Maturity thrust on him the need to disguise his dreams and dreamlife, the need to push on through in a world designed for others. Nights still swallowed him whole into far-off voyages, his sleep filled with intimacies his daylight life was barren of.

The journey home on Fridays was longer because Lékè stopped at Elias's shop on the corner of Nelson and Oxford. Over the past decade, the suburbs adjacent to trendy Observatory—Salt River and Woodstock—had gone through a process of re-development. Families that had lived in the area for generations were bought out by large developers and the wealthy. Main Road, running from Mowbray into the city center, was now a long commercial strip with low-rise apartment blocks, offices, fashion stores, galleries and restaurants. Organic food markets in old warehouses and light industrial buildings spread out from the main road towards Queen Victoria Street and the railway line. This creep of gaiety, however, ended abruptly at a set of traffic lights beyond which were a bunch of single-story houses arranged around a series of cul-de-sacs and one-way streets. Lékè lived here and Elias's store was just up the way. Rumor was that the shop was as old as Elias, that he'd been born there and any day now the old man would die there, leaving on the shelves, among the odd wares he sold, a half-empty stippled bottle of calamine lotion, an ornate bird cage with the wire door missing, and a multi-colored selection of unpackaged toothbrushes. At the entrance of the store was a basket full of socks. Keen customers who had been drawn in by the "R5 a sock" poster complained—the socks did not come in pairs. But Elias said socks didn't need to match if you were going to wear them with high boots.

Inside, in a corner of the shop, was a thin mattress where, during the day, Elias arranged his goods of scarves, shoes, and old collectable tins. At night he slept on the mattress with Whitie, the four-legged woman in his life. The Great Dane was eighty-four centimeters tall at the withers and just under one-ninety on her hind legs. Her shiny jet black coat ironically explained the choice of her name.

People wondered how Elias survived but, while most of his stock never seemed to move, he sold a great number of heavy duty black bags to a loyal group of customers; to those who cared to garden, he sold flower seeds.

Lékè stood at the entrance and stuck his head through the open door. "Elias?" he said.

"Yeah," Elias replied from somewhere out of sight.

Lékè stayed at the entrance, stretching his neck, looking in to the dark recesses of the room.

"Are you—"

"Come, come!" Elias shouted again.

"I'm in a hurry today," Lékè said into the shadows, shifting his weight from one leg to the other and still peering in. What he said had no bearing on his refusal to enter Elias's shop.

"Yes." Elias emerged from the darkness, standing by the corner, beckoning to his customer. "So come in, for God's sake!"

"No." Lékè shifted his weight again. "Can't stay, Elias."

"Whitie's in the back, Lékè." Elias now looked bored. "So come in."

Lékè stayed where he was. Elias went through to the back door and fiddled with the doorknob. Lékè understood this gesture was for his benefit. The week before, the back door had been closed but unlocked. The Great Dane had pushed through and frightened him. Today the door was locked—Lékè finally stepped into the shop. In the center lay a weary zebra rug that looked as if it had crawled into the middle of the space and died there. The ceiling was blackened from an old fire and a blue portable stove stood near the mattress. Everyone knew Elias used the stove to cook, but he insisted it was for sale. An orange sign with white lettering in the shop window had once claimed that everything inside had a price—including the shop owner. One day a woman from another neighborhood came into the shop and insisted she wanted to buy Whitie. After that Elias took the sign down.

Lékè stood behind the counter and asked for five packs of Four O'Clocks.

"Always the same thing, how come? Look, I've got Snapdragons, Sweet Peas, some Daisies." Elias pointed to pictures of various flowers pasted on the counter top.

Lékè shook his head. "Just the Four O'Clocks."

Elias shrugged and took five packs of the perennial seed out of a drawer. Lékè took a brown envelope from his backpack. In it was the money for the seeds. He placed the envelope on the counter and stared at it while he waited. The old man gave him the five packs and tucked one pack of Snapdragons into Lékè's top pocket. He began to protest.

"No, no, I insist. No charge. Just want you to spread out a bit." Elias winked. He enjoyed the young man's nervousness. He rubbed his thickened fingers over grey speckled jowls, wheezing from a lifetime of smoking. His hoarse laughter exposed yellowed teeth and a purple tongue. He was still laughing by the time Lékè was halfway up the road again.

At the front gate to his home, Lékè paused to catch his breath. He walked up the driveway and pulled out another brown envelope. He knocked on the front door.

"Who is it?"

It was a Victorian-style house. The grey roof shingles reminded Lékè of the scales of a fish. He imagined the tiles writhing. The pipes carrying the rainwater from the roof down to the gutters were made of copper. At the back of the house, a room had been added and to the side was the garage where Lékè stayed. He'd never been inside the house but he believed Widow Marais lived in the doorway. He imagined she had her whole life set up on the other side of the door that he knocked on every month. He made up a story that her husband had died of a violent disease and, in his last minutes of life, had run crazy through most of the house. The only part he never ran through was the doorway, so she moved her life into this threshold and was now waiting for her own death.

"Rent," Lékè shouted at the one-hundred-year-old hardwood door.

"Put it through," the widow screeched.

She was going blind and never left the house. Once a week, her niece came by, not on a visit of care, Lékè thought, but rather to see if her aunt had made it through another week. He heard the widow slap her cane against the flap in the door where the postman shoved the mail. Lékè pushed the envelope through, but didn't hear it hit the floor.

"Bye," Lékè said.

Widow Marais growled.

◀▶

A thick hedge grew alongside the house that divided the Marais compound into two unequal parts. Widow Marais's side was wild with overgrown bush. Lékè crossed onto his side, cutting through the hedge, careful not to scratch his ankles on the plant's thorns or damage his Woolworths trousers. If he hadn't needed to pay rent, he'd just have used his own private entrance. That was one of the things that had attracted him to the place. The advert had said: Small converted garage room. Separate entrance. R800 per month. Toilet. Shower. Sink. Available now. Phone Jeanine Marais. Lékè had phoned.

"Yes?"

"Um... I'm calling about—"

"Yes?"

"The garage room?"

"Still available. How old?"

"I...you mean–?"

"Age. Your age?"

"Twenty-five," he'd lied.

"Children? Pets?"

"No. No."

"Job?"

"Yes, I—"

"Where?"

Lékè gave her his manager's phone number. He'd been working there for almost a year and felt he could now afford to rent a place of his own. The next day Lékè called Jeanine Marais back as she'd asked him to.

"Fine," she said. "How soon?"

"One question," Lékè said which caused much silence on the other end; the widow seemed not to have given even a thought to the fact that her future tenant might have conditions of his own.

But in fact, it had been the reason Lékè had responded to her advert and if, on the call, she'd thought his condition odd, she hadn't cared enough to argue. The next day, Lékè moved into Widow Marais's "garage room," bringing all his possessions with him: his atlas collection, a small wardrobe of clothing, a mattress, a dark blue backpack, and Red—an old rusting Volvo 200 series stationwagon.

◆◆

The entire garden on Lékè's side had been plucked out and, as he walked, his half-worn brogues left muddied shoe prints on the rose-colored paving. A high wall ran the perimeter, protecting the space from the Cape Town winds; it created a stillness otherwise missing from the open streets. A wire gate, wide enough for a car to pass, broke the solidity of the wall and exposed the cul-de-sac beyond. Lékè entered his home. Inside, before his eyes could adjust to the darkness, he pulled a cord hanging by the door, and a fluorescent light buzzed. Lékè smiled at Red.

This had been the source of Widow Marais's confusion when Lékè asked if he could park his car inside the flat. Not in the driveway but actually inside.

"Wait, let me understand this," the widow had said in her strident tone. "I've spent a lot of money converting the garage into a room and now you want to turn it back into a garage?"

But she'd agreed.

Red had been Jane's car. Lékè remembered learning the word.

"Red," Jane would say, and point to the car.

"Red," Lékè would say back.

The name stuck.

When Jane died, Marcus parked the car to the side in the garage and there it stayed. But Lékè couldn't forget Red. The car conjured Jane in his memory, driving out to the flower farms and crowding the boot with pots of Clivias and Orchids. Back home, they transferred the plants into the garden while Marcus complained that Jane was using a decent car as if it were a wreck.

At eighteen, Lékè began the task of reviving Red. Marcus protested initially but stopped when Lékè ignored him. It took him a year, mostly due to having to save in order to buy the parts. Each month Marcus noted an added shiny piece, a dead part that now operated, a strong engine. When Lékè moved out, Marcus didn't stop him from taking Red—he couldn't recognize the car, anyway, since Lékè had started restoring it. Jane had been gone for eight years, the car had been sitting, rusting away all that time, and somehow Marcus had become accustomed to that. The restored car resembled exactly what Jane had driven but this didn't interest Marcus the way it seemed to obsess Lékè. In fact, on the contrary, it pained Marcus to see the red paint shiny again, to hear the engine working. Jane was gone; whether her car lived or died couldn't change that.

For Lékè, though, Red was not a painful memory, it was the spirit of something lost and he cleaved to it as if his life was determined by it. When Lékè returned to his new home after a Sunday drive with Red, he reversed through the wire gates, maneuvered the tight garage door, drove her right into the garage, hugged up against a wall, and positioned her with her nose facing outwards.

When he left for work in the mornings, on foot, he opened the left-hand-side doors. He didn't know what it was but he liked to come home and see her that way, open, somehow reaching out.

There was little else, the advert had been accurate. A shower, toilet, and sink. Lékè's mattress and a small fridge. Inside the fridge, a sachet of salt. On top of the fridge— three boxes of rusks, a stash of rooibos teabags, and a kettle. A small heap of clothing lay on the floor beside the mattress. His stack of atlases. The globes he'd stopped collecting in his teen years and left behind when he moved out, feeling perhaps that they belonged to a different time.

Lékè kicked off his shoes. He liked the cold of the floor and the feel of the grit that swept in through the gaps. The mattress creaked as he settled. It started to rain and he could hear the water hitting the roof, tinkling against the metal.

Lékè closed his eyes. When he opened them, the rain had stopped and it was dark outside. He shoved his feet back into his shoes and walked out onto the quiet street.

MONDAY 20TH JULY 1992

The baby was shifting again. Despite the coolness of the steel toilet seat, Elaine's upper lip was perspiring. She planted her feet on the floor and grabbed onto a bar to steady herself as she lifted up. The cramps had been go- ing since morning—intermittent—someone wringing out her intestines. She counted the days in her head: too early by almost a month. Should she call her doctor? Leave her post for a few minutes and use the public phones on the main road—Ursula could stand in for her and cash up? She checked: just enough coins in her pocket for the call. She washed her hands and ran her fingers over her forehead and cheeks.

"Need you out here, Elaine." Ursula cracked open the locker room door. "Long queue. Greyhound just pulled in. Boss says if you're not giving birth right this moment, get back to your post."

"Coming," Elaine said, but she stood studying her face in the mirror for a few seconds.

Vanguard Superette, owned by the Haddads, was

situated off the R300 along a major taxi route. It stood opposite a petrol station where several minibus taxi drivers
heading out of the Western Cape along the N2 stopped to
fill up their tanks and the passengers walked across to the
Superette to buy provisions for the road. At certain times
of the day, the Superette would crowd with urgent queues
at the checkout counters. Bus drivers would hoot from the
carpark, injecting panic through the store.

The excited energy of people starting or ending a
journey irritated Elaine—their often brusque manner at
the checkout counter always falling short of what she considered appropriate etiquette. People are rude, was her
grandmother's recurring lament.

The baby shifted again and she laid her hand on her
belly.

Outside the locker room, the lights hurt her eyes. She
could feel Bashir Haddad's hot stare on her neck as she sat
back on her stool and started serving the customers that
had gathered in her absence. She rang up the goods, not
bothering to look into people's faces.

She pulled items across the counter. A roll of toilet
paper. Two Maggie cubes. Tins of tomato puree.

"Wait. How much so far?"

Elaine looked up at her; skinny with a pink checkered
pinafore, the belt in a tight knot dangling on the side, she
wore a dirty white scarf. She wasn't a traveler; Elaine recognized her from the township nearby.

"Ten-forty-two," she replied and the woman slowly
took her hand off the rest of the contents in the basket.

A whole chicken. As Elaine pushed it through, a small
tear in the packaging widened. Pink chicken juice trailed
on the counter.

"Ag!" Elaine said as the blood dripped.

"Sorry," the customer said.

"It's not you. Look, use this, Ursh." She yanked a bag
from the box and shoved it at Ursula who, standing there
inspecting her nails, glared in response.

"Use a plastic first," Elaine added.

Ursula pulled a cellophane bag off the roll and eased the chicken into it. Then she placed it in the bright green grocery bag. Elaine continued ringing up the produce. Tinned corn—no name brand. The customer paid, taking a while as she counted out change from a plastic bank packet. She avoided looking at Elaine.

"Thank you," she said, taking the bag from Ursula and walking out of the store.

"Five kids. No husband," Ursula said, watching her go, then she went back to her nails.

At nine o'clock, the security guard shut the sliding doors and the last teller rang off.

"You in tomorrow?" Ursula asked Elaine at the end of the day as they gathered their things in the back room that passed for a staff room and store room, an everything room.

"No," Elaine said.

"When's it coming?"

Ursula gestured, snapping her fingers, and one of the new girls handed her a lighter. Her cigarette lit, Ursula threw the lighter into her handbag. The new girl frowned but didn't protest. Elaine watched the smoke rings form and disappear. In her time working at the store, she'd never seen anyone obey the "No Smoking" sign on the wall.

Ursula's cheekbones sharpened when she puckered her lips to send rings into the air. Rumors circulated that she was colored, passing for white, but Ursula wielded enough power to kill off the gossip.

Elaine pulled on her blue coat and checked the pockets for Oscar's letter, relieved by the touch of the tight roll of paper and the rubber band she'd snapped around it. She took a deep breath, inhaled the locker-room smell of shoe polish and corned beef. The strong odor pervaded every-thing including Elaine's coat which transferred the smell to her room when she hung it on the back of her bedroom door. At night she turned in her sleep, caught the scent, and frowned.

Elaine hung her straw bag on her shoulder and held her bulging stomach.

"It's a boy. One month still."

"I don't know how you cope."

Elaine winced. "We'll be fine."

"I mean," Ursula continued, stubbing out the cigarette and sticking it behind her ear, "who's going to play touch rugby with the boy? I've seen you, you can't throw. It's a shame, Elaine, man." And she sucked her teeth.

A woman sitting further down the bench crouched frozen over her laces, absorbing information for future gossip. Another lady washing her hands by the basin attempted to disguise her laughter.

"But you know, my Ouma always warned me about African men."

Elaine walked out.

The coat pulled tight around her chest but it no longer covered her stomach. Over the five years she'd worn it, one white button after another had popped off. She'd always meant to replace them.

By the time Elaine reached home, the temperature had dropped. Her toes were numb despite the heavy winter boots she wore and thick socks. A light drizzle had started and the baby was shifting again. She'd always imagined that babies in their mothers' wombs kicked but this one didn't, all he did was shift. It was different than kicking. Although she was sure of it, she couldn't explain how. The only person she'd tried to explain it to was Oscar and he seemed to understand.

"Shh, shh," Elaine hushed as she laid a hand on her stomach and unhooked the gate latch.

Stepping to avoid the rodent traps her landlady had set on the paving, Elaine made her way to the front door. She could barely feel her fingers, they were so cold, and it took a while to fish the house keys from her bag. The door opened easily after she turned the key and placed her weight against its wooden frame. A week's dishes jostled in the sink, fighting with cockroaches for space. The landlady had left a note with instructions on the kitchen counter. Elaine took off her coat. She placed her hands on her lower back and stretched, looking up at patches of the ceiling board sagging with brown crumbling pieces where the rain had come through.

She calculated how much time all the cleaning would take. There was the floor to mop and the cat had vomited a brown mush on the carpet. She'd try to get all the washing and ironing from last week done, aim for 1 am, and then sleep in a little. Her body was sore but it was a sensation to which she'd become accustomed.

Elaine tilted the blue bottle and as the milky liquid splashed into the bucket of water, a clean hospital smell filled the bathroom. She dug the balding mop in and, pushing the bucket along with her bare feet, she let it stand in the corner by the door. She took in a breath, swam her hands with a cloth down to the bottom of the full tub, and yanked the plug. It burped and farted as the body of water began to drain. Every few minutes, Elaine used the plunger to unblock the drain, pushing through caked dirt and chunks of hair. When the bath had emptied completely, a timeline of brownish streaks marked the sides. Elaine scrubbed them off.

He was shifting again.

"Shh, shh," she said and it came out hoarse and scratchy. A cockroach in the corner of the bathroom seemed to hear her and crawled away.

Elaine opened her eyes and closed them again. Already morning. Through the night, the wooden bed-frame had creaked at the joints as she'd moved, shifting her weight in search of a comfortable position. She'd struggled to fall asleep and was still awake at 3 am when her landlady came in. The sound of high heels and heavier footsteps in the passageway. Elaine had drifted off and woke to a sharp ache in her stomach; the skin over her belly felt as if it was ready to burst.

It was getting light outside, an early winter morning.

Knowing she'd never get back to sleep, Elaine rolled out of the bed. The floor was cold. She tiptoed to where she'd left her coat—the familiar bump of the rolled up letter in her jacket pocket.

My dear Elaine:

If I wasn't writing to you, if there wasn't a you for me to write to…It's so loud here, I can hardly think. Sometimes I can't feel myself. I mean, I can't hear myself. I don't know if I'm making sense. The sound of this place is harsh, really harsh. I can't sleep at night.

I'm OK though. Don't worry about me. Things could be much worse. I mean nobody bothers me, here. One of the gangs started asking me for information. Someone found out that I'm from the University. Now they call me Professor. They want information on their cases, they come to me with complaints, and they want ideas on how to decrease their sentences, the right words to use at their reviews. I don't dare tell them I'm not a lawyer and that I work in a chemistry lab. I can recite the periodic table backwards but my knowledge of the legal system is probably less impressive than theirs. I think on my feet though.

I like being called Professor. And I have a scar too. I think maybe that helps a little. You know the one, along the side of my ear? Who knows, maybe it's nothing to these men. God forbid they find out I didn't get it in a knife fight, that I got it racing my BMX down Road 9.

Did you get the money I arranged? How are you doing? How's that little boy in your stomach?

I dreamed he was born. You had him strapped to your back and you were singing a song, humming. I couldn't see your face, you were doing something at the sink. I could hear water and the sound of glass bumping. I put my hand on your shoulder and when you turned around, just before I saw your face, I woke up.

I must show you how to do that by the way—tie him to your back. I spent most of my childhood on my mother's back. The other women used to smile but my mother said it was the most sensible thing she'd been taught since she arrived in Ife. That, and how to make cornrows. She let my hair grow long as a baby and then she plaited cornrows all along my scalp. Women wanted to carry me, saying her daughter was cute; they argued with my mother when she said I was a boy.

Please continue writing to me. I want to know how you're doing. Send me a picture of yourself. And don't worry. Please don't worry.

I'm sorry. I love you.

Elaine read the letter through two more times. Then she tore a piece of lined paper from an exam pad.

Dearest Oscar:

I don't know how I'll wait for two years to see you. You know, with all that has happened, that seems the worst part of it. I'm sorry if that sounds selfish of me. Thinking of myself. It is, isn't it? It's selfish of me.

How are you? Thank you for your last letter. I keep reading it over and over again. When I read it, I hear the words in your voice.

I'm fine. Yes, I got the money, thank you.

You can stop worrying about me, I can take care of myself. The baby is fine.

Do you have ideas for a name? I thought something Nigerian. The girls at work will make fun of me but, I don't know, I thought something Nigerian would be good for him.

I miss you.

Love, Elaine

❦

The shower was cold, the geyser needed fixing, and Elaine's landlady had a stream of excuses for why it couldn't be done. Shivering, Elaine got dressed. Every now and then, she had to stop, hold onto the edge of her bed, doubled-over, until the pain subsided.

Her room was bare. Oscar's desk was the only piece of furniture she owned. The built-in-cupboard housed her modest array of clothes. She put on a wide dress she'd bought at a flea market; it was the one thing she felt comfortable in these days.

Oscar's desk had a flap that opened up like the desks she remembered from primary school. Inside she kept a copy of the Bible, Oscar's letters, and two photographs of herself—one when she was five holding her grandmother's hand, and another that Oscar had taken.

Elaine put the photograph away and went to the mirror, as if to check, to confirm that she was herself after all.

She touched her face. Her fingers lingered over the scars along her jaw and neck. Mostly, she didn't notice them. She'd learned, over the many years, to skip them. But now she looked, took everything in, allowed the memories. She remembered her grandmother's funeral, not in any detail. She'd been six years old at the time but even if she'd been older, it seemed to Elaine that the detail of that time would have anyway been wiped away by what came after. She did remember some things, in sharp bursts. She remembered black and perfume and old women in hats fixing their lipstick, fishing mints from out of their large handbags. Feathers would have been there at the funeral, surely, but she didn't remember him. The day he came to pick her up at the neighbor's (call him Uncle Malcolm, they said), that day was the first memory she had of his face. A wide face and white teeth. Elaine bared her teeth at the reflection in the mirror.

She heard her landlady click the front door, quickly finished dressing.

It must have rained in the night but despite a restless sleep, Elaine had not heard it. Her stomach churned as she walked along Main Road towards the post office, careful to avoid the puddles. The air smelled of rubber and dirt but there was also something comforting in the soft smell of fallen rain.

Her confrontation with the mirror and her memories fell away. At a corner on a skinny road off Main, a man in a beanie was arranging a table of fruit. She bought an orange, bit a hole in the top right through the orange skin and sucked—she hadn't eaten since the evening before.

The steps into the post office were slippery and Elaine was careful, leaned on the railing for support. Inside she joined the queue.

"Next." The woman behind the counter already looked tired.

There were only two open tellers. All the other windows had "closed" signs.

"Good morning," Elaine said. "I'd like to buy stamps please."

The postal worker had on thick glasses. She tapped the table top, indicating the slat in the glass partition, and Elaine pushed her letter through. She watched the woman take in her belly, read the address line on the envelope, another look at her belly.

"Is that the prison?" the woman asked, unnecesarily, thought Elaine, and louder than called for.

Elaine nodded. It was usually some combination of this. Today Elaine got a raised eyebrow as the woman pushed the stamps through.

"Next."

In her rush to leave—why did she feel, each time, that everyone had heard, that everyone was looking on, many Ursulas looking and passing judgment?—Elaine turned quickly; her haste blinded her and she charged straight into a thin woman, a bright orange hibiscus on the front of her shirt.

"Oh my God!" the woman shouted when she noticed Elaine's condition. "Did I hurt you?"

"I'm sorry," Elaine said. "It's me—I bumped into you."

"Are you OK, though?" The woman's eyes sparkled. "How far along are you?"

"Next!"

Elaine nodded and let the woman pass.

She found a surface to press on and began to lick the stamps. On visits to the post office, her grandmother would let her lick the stamps. As a little girl, she wondered why they put sugar on the back of stamps. To make the letter happier? To make it more special? Some stamps were sweeter than others. She got good at knowing which would taste like what. Much later, her grandmother told her about a neighbor who collected stamps. She couldn't quite imagine it. She never got the image out of her head—of an old man keeping stamps in a box, taking them out every few months to lick and taste them.

As Elaine walked out of the post office, something stabbed at her insides, forcing her to stand stock still in the doorway. She heard a distressing noise, realized it was coming from her own mouth.

She lost a sense of herself for a few seconds and when she came back to her own body, people were staring. The woman from before, with the hibiscus on her shirt, was close again and looking intently at her.

"I'm fine, I'm fine," Elaine said but as she spoke, a flow of liquid began slipping from between her legs. She looked down to see a clear puddle at her feet.

"Lady." The postal worker had left her seat. "That's your water breaking." The way she said it, Elaine wondered if she ought to apologize.

"Can we call someone?" hibiscus woman asked. "We need to call someone." Another contraction simmered and Elaine decided those questions were not meant for her. She felt a charge of anger towards this baby, coming like this, coming early. But then immediately she was sorry.

"I'm sorry," she said.

"What for, you didn't do anything," someone from the small group that had gathered said.

"I won't quite say that," some other disembodied voice replied. People laughed. People will always laugh.

Elaine reached for the edge of a counter nearby. She held firm. She felt if she let go, she might fall.

"Let me help you," hibiscus said.

"I'm...I..." She felt fuzzy, wanted to look in a mirror, just to see if all of her was all there. "I..."

"Ma'am? Ma'am, you're having your baby. Let me help you."

◆◆

Six hours later, a final burning sensation. In a sudden stream of slime and blood, he slipped out.

The midwife laid him, wet and wriggling, on her chest,

and although brand new, he seemed to fix Elaine with a stare. She remembered her irrational surge of anger towards him only hours before. "Sorry," she whispered. "You're here," she said. Then softer, "Hey, you're here."

She'd carried him and understood the biology involved but his presence in the room seemed miraculous, not logical, as if someone had picked him from a tree. She caressed his back, his legs, his feet. In fact Elaine was so absorbed in taking in her boy (each fingernail was there and complete), she didn't hear the door open.

"The nurse said I could come in. I told her you were my sister." Hibiscus smiled apologetically. She cocked her head at the baby. "He's perfect," she said. If she was surprised at the brownness of his skin, she didn't let on.

"I...I don't even know your name."

"Jane."

"Jane, thank you. For helping me, thank you so much."

"Can I?" Jane lifted the baby from Elaine's arms and held him aloft a few seconds, supporting his neck with her fingers. "So small," she said. "Do you have a name for him?"

"No, not yet. Soon, his father—"

"Oh—"

"—will...let me know. Soon."

"Well, hello you," Jane said to the baby. After a few minutes, she returned him to Elaine. "I ought to go."

"Of course. I'm sure I've taken over your whole day. I don't know how to thank you."

Jane shook her head. "No need to thank me, Elaine. I don't know why, I'm just happy to have been there today, in the post office. I'm happy to have...encountered you."

They smiled at each other. Seemingly on an impulse, Jane took a pen and scribbled something on a piece of paper.

"It's none of my business, Elaine, but...only if you need anything. I'll leave it here, call anytime."

"You're very kind," Elaine said and she meant it. An open kindness, not needling as she was accustomed. Such kindness had been so sparing in her life. She'd found it in

Oscar and now here again, in a stranger.

❦

Malcom Feathers—"Uncle Malcolm"—was a tight-lipped man. He said little to Elaine on that car ride away from the neighborhood she'd known all her life. She didn't know where he was taking her, only that he did so with the blessing of the neighbors; with her Grandma gone, he was the only family she had left in all the world. The neighbor's daughter, a few years older than Elaine, had said he was a rich man and that Elaine was lucky. She said Elaine would go to a fancy school, have a television in her bedroom, have a bedroom. She could eat whatever she wanted out of the fridge and she would no doubt learn to swim properly and travel to Disneyland.

None of these things would transpire quite as the girls imagined. And after much time had passed but before Elaine ran away, one day, tending to her wounds, she thought of Feathers and tried to imagine him as a little boy or even a baby cradled in someone's arms. She couldn't see it but this would become a kind of obsession. Always when her mind wandered, she would try and picture Feathers, swaddled, held. And now as she tried to nurse Lékè, she thought again. That she did so disturbed her greatly but she couldn't stop the familiar obsession from creeping up. Strangely enough, she could see it. She could see that Feathers, evil as he was, had once too been someone's child.

❦

The hospital helped Elaine put a call through to Oscar. She asked if he was sitting down not because she meant it literally just that she'd heard it said in the movies and she liked the feeling of drama the moment carried. After his initial whoops of delight, Oscar settled down and there was silence on the line.

"Your son looks just like you," Elaine said. When he didn't say anything, she said, "Oscar?"

"I was supposed to be there."

"You were." She knew it was silly at this stage to indulge in romance but went on anyway, because there would only be one day like that, one day when their son would be born. "You were here and you're here now."

"How are you doing?"

"I'm fine. We're both fine."

"What's he doing now?"

Elaine looked down at the baby. "Frowning." She laughed.

Later, in her dream, Elaine was on a bus and her stomach was cramping. Everything was dark but she knew there were other people on the bus with her. Suddenly she got up and asked the driver to stop. Outside there was a tree with a wide trunk. She climbed and settled herself in the branches, lay back, spread her legs. The surges of pain came and receded. She could hear drumming. The pain intensified and then stopped for good. Her legs spread wide, a small head, spindly feet, and wet feathers inched down her cervix and out her vagina.

"Oh," the bird said when they locked eyes. "It's you."

As it spread its wings, Elaine shielded her eyes from the fierce yellow light.

⊷⊷

The hospital kept her for an extra day. The baby caught jaundice and his eyes were bandaged while he was placed beneath a bright lamp that Elaine worried would scorch his skin. Oscar called.

"It's perfectly normal," he said. "I've heard of that happening; he'll be fine."

Elaine told him her dream.

"Hmmm."

"What?" She felt a sense of panic. "Is it good?"

"He recognized you. He chose you, so he is where he belongs—no mistake has happened."

Elaine nodded—she'd not thought about it that way.

"But he flies away so maybe he'll leave us."

"Don't talk like that, Oscar."

"Come on, Elaine. It's a good thing. Children are supposed to leave their parents. To have better lives. Easier lives."

"I just don't want any sadness around him. I want happy stories."

"Yes. My father used to tell me stories—not all of them were happy, but still they made me feel safe. And he used to sing to me."

"Have you got a name yet? I need to sign the birth certificate."

"Well, I was thinking...Lékè."

"Lay-kay."

"It was my father's name."

"Lékè."

"It means...Ĩfálékè, it means Ifa triumphs. Lékè is to triumph."

"I like that. Triumph. Yes." Elaine was silent for a while. Then she asked, "Was he happy?"

"What?"

"Was your father a happy man? I'm sorry, I don't mean to—"

"Yes! Yes, my father was a very happy man."

She relaxed. "You said he used to sing to you."

"Babaláwo mo wá bẹ̀bẹ̀..."

"I like the sound of that."

"It's a story. My father used to tell me many stories."

◇◇

That night Elaine drifted into a half-sleep, her mind aware of her new baby next to her, his soft breathing. She felt weighed down by an invisible mass. Her stomach ached and in between her legs was a throbbing sensation as though blood was gushing. But her clothes were dry. She thought she heard Oscar's voice in her sleep, imagined he'd been released and was standing beside her singing to Lékè. She wanted to ask him something but sleep held her back.

Something startled her and she awoke with a fright. For a second, with the morning light sneaking through the blinds, she didn't know where she was. The hospital TV was on mute but she could hear voices coming from the passageway, the squeak of wheels rolling on the floor. She thought of Oscar far away in a prison cell. Lékè was still in the white crib beside her bed, an arm's length away.

Elaine put her hand to her chest. She exhaled audibly, just as a nurse entered the room.

"Everything OK, Elaine?"

"Yes." She had to pat her chest to keep from crying. "Yes, everything is fine."

"Let's try again."

The nurse helped Elaine with the baby. Lékè was struggling to latch. Once in position, the nurse left them alone and Elaine drifted asleep. She awoke to find Lékè asleep, his mouth on her raw nipple. She slept again and woke, empty-handed, with a start. But the baby was right there, in the bassinet. The nurse must have come back and moved him.

Elaine tried to be still, tried to listen to the sound of his breathing.

◈◈

"I'm writing to him."

"What do you mean?"

"Letters."

"He's just a baby, Oscar!"

"I know, I know. When will he be able to read? Not just ABC, when will he be able to really understand things?"

"What are you talking about?"

"They're for him to read."

"Yes, and you can wait and tell them to him, face to face."

"It's too long. He'll need something in the meantime."

Elaine was silent. They seldom spoke so plainly about Oscar's sentence. It was as if they were immune to time. Finally she said, "I'll bring him to see you."

"No!"

"Oscar."

"No, Elaine. I don't want that. He'll be two by the time I get visiting rights. I don't want him here. This is no place for a baby."

She wanted to protest but also she felt sad for the end

of their fantasy. Here they were in a real conversation and time and the rules of time applied.

"It's filthy here, Elaine. And the smell... don't bring him here, please. Don't ever do that."

"But—"

"I don't care. Don't come to visit with him. Please."

Elaine heard a voice in the back, gruff and short.

"I have to go."

"A boy needs his father, Oscar," Elaine whispered, looking to the couch where she'd put Lékè down.

She'd started work again, but she didn't know how to tell Oscar the money was gone, spent.

"Please, Elaine," Oscar continued. "It'll be better that way. I can't let him see me like this. I can't let him remember this."

"He won't. He'll be too young."

"Doesn't matter. This is not the place for him. I'll be out, you'll see, the time will pass quickly. You'll see."

Oscar's lie polluted the phone call. Elaine felt, strangely, that she wished not just to put the phone down but to throw it away altogether.

SATURDAY 25TH JULY 1992

Dear Lékè:

"Am I Nigerian?" I asked my dad. He nodded.

"And I'm South African too?" My mother nodded.

"How come we don't go there? And how come your skin is like that but Daddy and me are like this?"

"Daddy and I."

"If you're really my mother, how come you're oyinbo?"

They never answered my questions so I decided to try ignoring theirs too.

"Oscar, where are your school socks?"

I nodded and got a smack from my mother.

"Why did you bite Tèmílàdé?"

I feigned as best I could the smile I'd seen too many times on their faces. My father gave me a lecture and sent me to my room.

Later he would come to get me, while my mother went to bed. NEPA would have turned off the electricity. A naked candle poking out of a Star beer bottle, the wax dribbling over the blue label.

Babaláwo mo wá bẹ̀bẹ̀.

If he'd already had a bit to drink, he would be impatient with my bad pronunciation as I tried to repeat the words.

"What are they teaching you in school?" and "All that English with your mother all day—what a mistake. I told her to let me take you to Èkìtì!"

I loved my father. Maybe because he really talked to me, albeit he may have let slip what my mother referred to as "inappropriate details." The point is, he spoke freely to me and I felt important.

"Bom Boy! Come here, jo! Let me tell you a story."

He shouldn't have called it a story. He didn't have to pretend with me—I worked it out eventually, I knew.

FRIDAY 27TH JULY 2012

Lékè pushed the buzzer. The camera flashed and he knew Marcus had seen and recognized him. The steel gates parted and as he pulled into the driveway and switched off Red, he wished he hadn't agreed to come. He hated coming back here. He locked the car doors even though this was the safest house in Cape Town.

It hadn't always been like this. Marcus's fervor for locks, padlocks and security cameras came after Jane's death. Lékè would return home to an added security measure or to tradesmen trying to convince a compliant Marcus to bulk up on something he hadn't needed in the first place.

Lékè watched Marcus unwrap the take-away parcels. He pushed the white plastic bags, damp from steam, to the side of the kitchen table and pulled the cardboard tops off the foil containers. The smell of steaming curry and basmati rice filled the kitchen. Marcus's bony hands twitched, hands with reddish-brown marks across the white skin, wrinkled. He wiped them on his black trousers.

"Let's eat," Marcus said, looking up at Lékè, who got

two plates from the cupboard, pulled cutlery from the basket near the sink.

They settled at the table although Lékè knew Marcus,
as a rule, ate in front of the television when he was alone.
He'd come home one evening and found him eating pizza,
watching the National Geographic channel through his
wire spectacles. Lékè had sat beside him as he switched
channels to Animal Planet and then BBC, back and forth,
shovelling the pizza slices into his mouth. It had seemed
reckless. Dirty plates and bowls with hardened brown
specks spread across the rug and underneath the set-
tee—each dish at a different stage of decay. Marcus hadn't
shaved in a few days and white shoots covered his chin.

"Happy belated birthday, son," Marcus said, setting
down his fork.

Lékè's face remained flat, expressionless.

"Here." Marcus raised his wine glass and the gold liquid
caught the light from the hanging pendant.

The clink of their glasses struck but then the silence
took over again.

Marcus shifted in his seat. "I... there's something I want
you to have. Well, Jane always, you know, kept it... she
asked me to make sure you get it... at the right time."

Lékè put his fork down, the contents of his plate mostly
untouched.

"It's for you from....from before—"

"I don't want it." Lékè frowned.

He'd watched Marcus pull the envelope from a pile of
innocent-looking mail.

"Give it a chance, Lékè."

"No. I don't want it." He picked up his fork but put it
down again. "I don't want anything from before, I've told
you. I need to go. Thanks for dinner."

He rose from the table and left the kitchen. Marcus
didn't protest. The bang of the front door, the sound of Red
pulling away, and he was alone again.

The large house in which his son had once pored over
his atlases seemed to swell to twice its size after Jane's

death. It gobbled up the sound of Lékè's feet stamping the old wooden floors; the sound of his laughter as he splashed in the bathtub calling for her to play with him.

Although he was never much of a talker, for three months after her death, Lékè had stopped speaking completely. At first Marcus, occupied with his own grief, did not notice. He worked late in his damp-smelling office at the University, crowding his mind with an unrelenting series of minute facts. He started a paper on trace fossils and radiometric dating and got lost in the pre-historic past, seduced by relics. Silent data, he called it. He liked this—the quiet stories of rocks, no words, just markings and lines. No wonder Lékè's loss of speech did not register for Marcus; in a way, he'd lost his too.

In those days soon after the funeral, it became a habit for Marcus to arrive home late. The babysitter would be sleeping on the couch with the TV on mute. Marcus would turn it off and touch her on the shoulder.

"Oh," she'd say with a start. It was always the same. She'd sit up and rub her eyes. "I didn't hear you come in, sir."

Marcus paid her and walked her out to her car. Back inside, he turned off all the lights in the house and meandered through as if he were visiting a museum. He didn't cry, but he put his index finger between his teeth and bit down. Before going to bed, he passed through Lékè's room—stopped a while to watch him sleeping—collected blankets from the cupboard and settled in front of the television. In those days, the couch was the only place he found a good night's rest.

❦❦

Lékè didn't want anything from before. In fact, he didn't want anything. Marcus had called him on his birthday and he hadn't picked up. But then he'd kept calling and it became difficult for Lékè to ignore him. Now as Lékè drove home, he regretted agreeing to visit. Lékè hated to stand in the house, to look at Marcus; it hurt his eyes although he couldn't explain why. Something to do with the last ten years, and the big expanse that had stretched out between him and Marcus, wide and silent. And Jane gone, nothing between them to soften the echo.

◄►

After that day with the photograph of the strange woman with the fancy table cloth and Jane home from hospital—year after year, she'd gotten worse.

"Why are you home?" Lékè asked Jane when he returned from school on his bike, not to the usual company of the housekeeper, Lightness, but to Jane in her bathrobe, face gaunt.

"To keep you company." She smiled, not having to bend too low to hug him.

"You're sick again?"

"No, sweetheart. Just tired."

Lékè knew she was lying. "Where's Marcus?"

"Daddy's gone away on a conference for the weekend. So it's me and you."

They stayed outside. Spring had eased away for the kind of harsh sunny days Jane adored and Lékè tolerated. They'd sat on the veranda, Jane going on—in between pauses where she caught her breath—about the flowers she would plant before the December holidays.

"Star jasmine, right there, Lékè, by the front door."

She pointed at it as if he'd never walked through it before, never seen it. And he too, he looked. They smiled at each other.

"And maybe another vegetable patch to the side there, away from those hungry rubber tree roots. Goodness, I might have to get someone to chop it down."

"No!"

"I know, I love it too, but look how it gorges itself. If we're not careful, it'll uproot the whole house."

After a short silence, Lékè'd asked, "What else?"

"I've been thinking of a perennial maybe?"

Lékè frowned. "Thought you didn't like them."

"Perennials?"

"You said. That time at the show. That they're fakes."

Jane laughed out loud. "I must have been in a bad mood."

Lékè looked unconvinced. "You said they lived on and on and that's not real life."

Jane didn't respond immediately. She looked beyond the rubber tree and head-height bougainvillea hedge that separated her garden from the neighbor's. "I think I've changed my mind," she said finally. "Besides it's the Mirabilis jalapa."

"The—"

"Four O'Clocks. They open when the temperature drops in the evening and by morning they wilt. Perennial." She frowned. "Kind of."

That weekend Jane agreed and Lékè came into her and Marcus's bed, slept curled against her in a way he hadn't done since he was a little boy. Jane embarrassed him when, in a moment, she cupped his cheek. In the morning, Lékè woke up shivering, the bed was damp.

"Mum?"

"Water," Jane said. Her lips were wrinkled. "Some water, please."

When he returned, Jane was staring up at the ceiling.

TUESDAY 5TH NOVEMBER 2002

A month after Jane's death, the Western Cape Earth Science Club invited Marcus to give a series of lectures on his speciality, trace fossils within the Precambrian period. He enjoyed the challenge of working within the span of this era, a field where fossil records were poor yet it accounted for eighty-seven percent of geological time.

"Knysna," Marcus mouthed as he put down the invitation. They'd got married there. He checked the dates again. The trip was ten days long and he felt guilty at his eagerness to get away. He called the number on the invitation and accepted.

It was an amateur palaeontology institution and they offered a small stipend, room and board. The town was mostly overcome with holiday makers but there were a few people who were attending the conference. Several had heard of Professor Marcus Bisset, had read his papers in journals. The caress of academic success was a welcome distraction. He sent Lightness a text when he arrived and called home two days later.

"He's not talking, sir."

"What's the matter? Is he upset?"

"No. He's just not talking. His teacher called to say they were sending him home."

"What happened?"

"He's not talking. When they call his name in class, he says nothing."

Marcus looked out the window. There was a church across from his boarding house, not the one they'd said their vows in but—

"Where's he now? What's he doing?"

"I left him in his room, he's looking through his books, those books of his, the maps."

"Put him on the phone."

"You didn't say goodbye to him. I told you that would cause trouble with a child."

"He's hardly a child, Lightness. I left him a note, I needed to beat the traffic."

Lightness made a sound of disapproval.

"Put him on the phone."

He waited while she put the phone down. The Zimbabwean woman had worked for Jane's sister, raising her four kids. By the time they decided to adopt Lékè, the kids had grown up and left the house. Two lived in Canada, one emigrated to Australia, and the other lived in Durban. Jane was not particularly close to her sister but she was offered Lightness as a "life saver." On meeting her during a large family reunion, Marcus was immediately jealous of the easy way Lightness had with both adults and children.

He heard someone pick up the receiver. "Hello? Lékè, it's Dad!"

There was no response.

"Lékè!" he sang, trying something he'd heard Jane do.

"You cannot raise a child over the phone, sir."

"Put him back on, Lightness."

"Haven't you heard me? He's not talking. When are you back? You must come now."

"I don't think it's such an emergency."

"I just give him food when I think he's hungry. I don't know what he's thinking. I don't want to leave him alone in his room at night. He needs you, sir."

How strange, Marcus thought as he wiped his eyes, his hands temporarily obscuring the view of the white church—to come all this way to cry.

"Sir?"

He cleared his throat. "Soon. I'll be there soon, Lightness."

◆◆

He stayed in Knysna for the duration of the conference, calling home every two days to find out that nothing had changed.

He started his drive back to Cape Town after 2 pm and stopped in Swellendam to spend the night, telling himself that driving in the dark was a bad idea. The following day he set out late again and arrived back in Cape Town at dusk. Driving into town along the N1, he ignored the men selling car phone chargers and wire versions of "The Big Five." He dropped his speed to avoid the hidden cameras and, after passing the Pinelands off-ramp, turned towards the University, putting off arriving home, hoping Lékè would be asleep by the time he got back.

If anything, Marcus had missed the campus and his office. He stood in the doorway for a few seconds then switched on the lights and ran his fingers over the hulking books on his desk, two massive rocks as book ends.

On the way home from the University, he stopped at the ATM. Lékè was asleep when he arrived, Lightness fraught with worry.

"What are you going to do?"

"Nothing. You can leave now, I'll be fine."

"Nothing? This child needs help, sir. A normal doctor, or even I can take him to my doctor."

"Oh please, we don't need that charade again."

In the last stages of her sickness, Lightness had convinced Jane to allow her sangoma to bless and guide her.

"It's not a charade."

"I'm his father. I say he's fine."

She picked up her bag.

"I have something to give you." He handed her a thick envelope, which she took, looking confused.

"Sir?"

He cleared his throat.

"What's this?" she asked.

"I think it's better if we...I think it's—"

"I won't leave him. I've done nothing wrong."

"Please. Don't make this difficult. I need to be alone."

"What of the boy? What does he need?"

"He needs me, you said so yourself. I promise I'll take care of him."

She left, water running from her nose.

Marcus walked through the house. The door to Léke's room was cracked open and he could hear a strange shuffling. He pushed the door open and found Léke, his back to the door, playing on the floor. Marcus had seen him playing this strange game before—sitting with his legs open, tearing strips of white paper and twisting the strips and then shuffling them around on the floor. The box of Legos that Marcus's sister had brought for him remained unopened in the corner. Marcus stood still for a while in the doorway. He sighed and stepped into the room.

"Hey there." He walked towards the bed and hugged Léke. "How are you?" he asked.

"Fine," Léke said.

"Ah! So you do speak after all. What was all the fuss about?" Marcus smiled but Léke just disentangled himself from the awkward embrace and returned to his game. "Bedtime, my boy," Marcus said, his smile disappearing and a heavy sense of fatigue settling onto his shoulders.

Lékè didn't resist. He was already dressed in his pajamas. He climbed into bed.

"Good night," Marcus said.

"Good night."

Lékè spoke only when Marcus spoke to him so Marcus
came home earlier in the day to engage with the boy.
Slowly, he invited friends around and, over the course of
four months, Lékè was willing to answer any question put
to him. He rarely volunteered conversation but that, Marcus
decided, was simply the child's personality. Relieved to
have cured Lékè and relieved to have been extracted from
what had seemed like a trance-like ritual of work and home
with little or no contact with anyone in between, life-after-
Jane continued for Marcus, boring and unremitting.

FRIDAY 31ST JULY 1992

For Lékè:

Babaláwo mo wá bèbè

I remember when I asked my father what that meant.
First, the regret in his eyes that my Yoruba was so useless.
Well, whose fault was that really? Anyway, I told him I knew
what Babaláwo meant, but what about the rest?

The song tells the story of Ìjàpá, the tortoise, whose
wife, Yóníbō, cannot bear children. On the advice of a
neighbor, Ìjàpá travels through a forest and visits the home
of Babaláwo, the Ifa diviner, to ask for guidance.

The Babaláwo listens to his plight and performs the
necessary rituals. She gives Ìjàpá a bowl of soup that he is
to give to his wife to drink the minute he arrives home.

Ìjàpá leaves his offerings and starts the journey home,
the Babaláwo's warnings ringing in his ear—don't drink the
soup, it is for your wife.

I loved the story and, to prolong it, I would find ways to
interrupt my father.

I'm four. I'm high up, each leg dangling off my father's
broad shoulders. We must be going to the farm because
I'm wearing my blue rubber boots—I remember they were
heavy to walk in—and when I look down, the ground is far

away. We cross a bridge, avoiding where the slats are beginning to rot and give way. It has rained. I make my father
promise to take me fishing. He never did but in that moment, right there, I was safe.

I didn't finish telling you the rest of the "Babaláwo
story."

The journey home through the forest was long and arduous for Ìjàpá. It was Harmattan season and the dry winds
parched his skin and throat. Almost faint from exhaustion,
he stopped under a dried out tree and drank the tantalizing
soup. Arriving home, he assured Yóníbō the medicine had
been in the form of incantations and that it would soon start
to work. Within days, Ìjàpá's belly became engorged and
an acute pain consumed him. Concerned, Yóníbō decided
to take him to the Babaláwo for a cure. As they walked,
Ìjàpá sang:

Babaláwo mo wá bẹ̀bẹ̀ Alugbinrin
Mo bojú wo kùn ó rí gbendu, Alugbinrin
Babaláwo mo wá bẹ̀bẹ̀, Augbinrin

In Ìjàpá's song, he confessed his greed and suppli-
cated the Ifa priest. Yóníbō suddenly understood what had
happened. When they arrived in front of the Babaláwo,
she offered no pity, citing that she had warned Ìjàpá. He
writhed in pain and died in the arms of his wife.

Of all the stories, Lékè, this was my favorite. And somehow, in the way that he told it, I felt it was the one in particular that my father wanted me to remember. My mother
was often irritated; my father, wobbly on his feet, would pull
me close and she'd sigh—Not another story, Lékè, she'd
say. Did I mention my father's name was Lékè? Not another
one, Mum would say. Dad would whisper for me not to mind
her but he didn't need to. I understood what she did not.
It wasn't just another story. He was giving me something.
That's how it is, Lékè.

MONDAY 6TH AUGUST 2012

Right at the edge of Lékè's suburb, a new shopping
center opened. It soon became his habit to visit. He walked

the route to the back of the mall and slipped in through a delivery door. During the day, this access was busy, but after 6 pm, it got quiet. He entered under the bright lights of the mall, squinting but enjoying the glint on the tiled walls. The crowds surprised him but he remembered seeing a flyer announcing that stores were open till 10 pm to test out the late-night shopping market.

The Plaza Mall smelled of paint and brass polish. From the high ceilings, warm colored lights hung low, and along the floors elaborate clay pots held palm fronds and cacti, the curves of the snake plant.

All the shoppers in the mall seemed to Lékè in a dance, an intricate dance that started when they entered the mall and ended as they left. The mall was hypnotic, like an enchanted forest, but instead of trees and bushes, there were elevators and escalators, and in place of animals, there were sales people. Instead of fruit, clothes sprouted in the shop windows, waiting to be picked.

Lékè wandered into a department store.

"'Scuse me, how much for this?" a shopper asked.

Her plum red hair, Lékè noticed, was grey at the roots. She had a walking stick, which she leaned on with her ring-clad right hand. In her left, she dangled a shiny red belt, shaking it at the sales assistant like a snake she'd caught. Lékè busied himself to one side of the store, turning the metal stand with silk scarves hanging from the hooks. The assistant took the belt and examined it.

"There is no price tag, that's why I asked you."

"Of course, sorry." The assistant handed it back and, from his counter, made a phone call.

While she waited, the woman tried on the belt. She tied it around a thickened waist and turned from side to side to examine the effect in front of a full length mirror.

"What do you think?" she turned and asked Lékè.

He pretended not to hear and, his heart pounding, walked out of the shop. She'd caught him off guard. Usually he managed to blend into the background and no one ever noticed him. He regretted not answering back. Scolding himself, he waited down a passageway leading to the toilets and saw the woman walk past with the designer carrier bag, her purchase inside.

Lékè followed her through the mall but he worried she'd recognize him. At the cosmetics store, he watched her try on three shades of lipstick before he left.

After half an hour of aimless wandering, another woman caught his attention. Her hips swung out when she walked. She was wearing spiky heels, the kind with which, he imagined, you could pierce a hole in someone's neck. She was younger than the first woman with the belt, and bustier too. Along her brown fleshy arms, she wore silver bangles. Lékè followed her. He was there when she took too quick a step and fell, making a loud whoop as she landed on her bum. A group of teenagers giggled. Lékè rushed to assist her, helped her collect the scattered belongings.

"Thank you."

He smiled a response.

Later, on his walk back towards the house, he slipped the lone bangle from underneath his sweater. It was slender and delicate and he remembered how she had pushed it up along to the thicker part of her arms so that the silver dug into her flesh. He forced the bangle up his bicep, enjoying the tightness of its hold on his skin.

The December after Jane's death, Lékè planted the perennials she'd mused about, but they only blossomed the following year. Every two years he planted a new batch so that when one plant was dying, another was blooming. When he moved out, he took cuttings from the Four O'Clocks she'd planted in what he still thought of as "Jane's garden." He'd hoped that the small patch of ground at the back of his studio would be completely his own but Jane still filled the space. He pretended she wasn't there but she stood behind him while he worked, telling him not to plant the seeds too close and not to overdo it with the mulching.

There was no outside light at the back, but a moon cast down giving the garden a muted glow. Lékè stood surveying the results of his work. Along one side was a window into Widow Marais's house, but it was frosted glass, nothing to be seen. Along the other two sides of the garden were high walls. He'd divided the ground into three beds: one planted with rows of Four O'Clocks at ruler-height, the bright blossoms open and oozing a sweet scent; in another were spindly stems, little babies shooting out of the ground. Lékè, barefoot, bent down and continued work on the last bed, pulling up a run of dead daisies and tough grass growing in the corner against the wall. He'd put on his gardening shorts so he could kneel on the ground without dirtying his work clothes. Using a fork, he began to turn the soil, inhaling the smell he'd come to love over the years working beside Jane. He mixed in the compost he'd picked up from Elias and started to dig out a small ditch. He could fit in three lines. The garden soil was soft and compliant from the rain. He used his fingers to dig out space for new seeds. He took the packet, tore it open, and poured a few seeds into his palm, walking along the run and placing them in the holes he'd dug. Jane had taught him to collect garden refuse in a specific part of the garden, keep it there, steaming, ready for use when necessary. Lékè took the tin bucket he'd found neglected in Widow Marais's bushy garden. It had a small hole in the side but it was perfect for moving soil or mulch. Filling it with the garden refuse he'd collected over the months and some extra bark Elias had given for free, he spread it over the bed. The mulch fell with soft thuds and Lékè thought of blankets, and of Jane kissing him goodnight.

"Shh, shh," he whispered and afterwards wondered who he was talking to.

WEDNESDAY 19TH AUGUST 1992

My dear Elaine:

How are you? Thanks for the photograph in your last letter; I remember the day I took it.

How is Lékè? I can't believe he's almost a month old. Even though I'm tired, when I think of him, I notice that I smile. But when I smile, there is also a pain in my chest. Life has confused me.

I've noticed I feel tired a lot. Not when I'm speaking to you on the phone, then I'm most awake! It's this place, I feel as if I'm always holding my breath, clenching my teeth, my fists. I wake up tired.

Sorry to say these things.

I'm OK, really. I'm mostly left alone here. I'm grateful, but not everyone shares my fortune. I am now in a cell with forty other men. Some of them are just boys, really.

I'm scared, Elaine. I might get lost here. Write to me.

◆◆

Elaine didn't intentionally skip a week without writing or phoning but when she came home from work and collected Lékè from her neighbor, the time to sit and write seemed to elude her. In the morning, she expressed milk and then hurried to drop Lékè off. Telkom had cut the phone-line and her landlady installed a pay as you go. Rather than spend the money on the call, Elaine bought bread.

◆◆

The smell of semen and urine comes through my dreams. I wake up gagging.

I sleep with my head by the wall. "Poes," someone has written, as if they are talking to me. There are also pictures. A vagina with a speech bubble; I cannot make out the words.

I missed your letter last week; perhaps it got lost in the mail.

I continue with my letters to Lékè. I'll send them with this one to you. I'll put them in a separate envelope.

My mattress stinks. It's sweat. Each night, as a distraction, I lie down and pretend you're beside me. Your lavender smell.

How is Lékè? Kiss him for me. I put a mental picture of him under my pillow. I sleep better that way.

I've spoken to my lawyer about the money the University still owes me. I think it will all be sorted out soon. I have asked her to send you something in the meantime. I'm so sorry, Elaine, I cannot undo this.

Love always,

Oscar

◆◆

What was it about letters from Oscar that had her standing in front of a mirror? Elaine turned sideways, noticing the small bulge still around her waist. She smoothed her shirt down her front, holding her stomach in, and leaned closer, studying first one side of her face and then the other.

◆◆

In prison, Elaine's letters were more human to Oscar than the men he shared a cell with. The letters kept him sane, a kind of necessary course of medicine that he needed to stay alive. When he missed a letter, he could feel his blood slug through his veins, uninterested. He lost his appetite and the environment around him, violence and loneliness, seemed normal. Sometimes he panicked and re-read her old letters but it didn't help so much.

On nights when he could not fall asleep, he traced back, looking, thinking maybe somewhere in their connection would be a clue he missed for this current reality, him in prison, Elaine at home with a son he had yet to see and touch.

◆◆

"Oh, excuse me," the woman said. "They'd said this room was empty. I would've knocked."

Oscar had noticed her before, wearing the distinct bright blue and red cleaner's uniform, walking the passageways of his department. She was a small woman, pale with liquid- grey eyes. The reason he'd first noticed her was because she was so short. He'd seen her from behind once, thought she was one of the lecturer's children, wondered if perhaps she was lost. Despite lugging around the mop in a heavy steel bucket, she looked as though you could scatter her with a puff of wind—what were those things called again? Oscar remembered them from the farm. Just a puff and off they went.

"No problem. You're actually right. I was meant to be giving a tutorial. But you see some of the students complained to the faculty head that they can't understand my accent. Do I sound like I'm speaking English to you?" Oscar felt bad, but why should he not unburden himself?

The woman shifted her weight then said, "I'll come back then."

"No no no! Come in, please. Don't let me stop you."

She hesitated then entered the office.

Oscar's desk was set against the back wall, facing the door. To the left of the desk was an aging wooden cabinet with dusty glass doors holding back a stack of books. Something about the books seemed restless; some of them had pages that, swollen with age, had spilled from their dried out spines. Some pages had fallen and were stuck between the glass doors. When Elaine opened the cabinet doors to clean them, the pages fell onto the ground, sending the dust into the air.

Oscar sneezed.

"Bless you."

"Thanks." He tried marking scripts but, distracted, kept looking up.

"What's your name? I'm Oscar."

"Elaine."

"Ah, pleased to meet you."

She crossed to the right of the desk and began cleaning the heavy wooden-framed windows. She worked quietly but every few minutes let out a low hum, a piece of a song. Each time she did this, Oscar looked up. She had her back to him. The red sash of the uniform fit round her small waist and ended in a bow with long ties that fell over the swell of her backside. She was small, but she was definitely a woman.

Elaine turned around and caught him staring at her. A warm flush rose from the base of her neck to her temples. Simply looking away didn't diminish Oscar's embarrassment, and he emitted a series of coughs, hoping the brash sound would do the trick.

"I need to vacuum. Should I come back?"

"Listen. It's fine. I'll go. I can finish this at home." He rose and started packing away the papers into his briefcase.

"Sorry for the trouble," she said.

"No trouble."

Elaine stood as he fumbled with the buckle of his worn leather bag. He glanced at her sideways. "How's the bicycle? The, um, the tire?"

She looked confused.

"I saw you the other day pumping it up. Did you manage to fix it?"

"For now, yes, but...I've already patched it twice."

"I wouldn't compromise on that if I were you. Just get a new one, they can't be that expensive." A few more seconds of silence passed before Oscar guessed that his candor had somehow offended her. "I didn't mean to say... what I mean is...I'm sorry." He felt unclear about what he was apologizing for.

Elaine's mouth set firm. She looked down. Oscar apologized once more and left the office.

◆◆

He drove home, sitting at the green robot until the car behind him hooted. His earlier confrontation with his students was forgotten. He enjoyed remembering as much detail as he'd managed to take in during their short encounter. Her hands would fit inside his. A strong scent he couldn't place.

The following day, walking on University Lane, he realized what the scent was. He veered towards the bush that bordered the paved lane. Lavendar. He picked a sprig and kept it in his pocket.

The next time Oscar saw Elaine, it was six o'clock on a Friday evening. He'd walked into the senior lecturers' common room and found her paging through one of the fiction novels on the shelf. She didn't hear him enter. He walked quietly and, leaning over her shoulder, said, "Most of the book is tedious but there's a great sex scene on page one hundred and twenty."

Elaine blushed.

"I'm sorry. I've done it again. I'm an idiot..."

"No. It's fine." Her hands were shaking as she turned to put the book back.

"Why don't you keep it? Take it for the weekend. Read and...maybe tell me what you think."

"No! No, thank you. I need to get to work." She walked around him, picked up her mop and bucket at the entrance to the room, and left.

❖❖

In bed that night, Oscar lay awake. Despite her size, Elaine wore the serious face of an adult, unlined but stiff. Her hair was short and just where the brown strands ended along the base of her neck, the skin thickened and had the color of dried grass—some kind of injury.

A couple of weeks passed before he saw her again. He went to find her in the locker room assigned to the cleaners.

"I have something for you."

"What?"

One other cleaner was in the room. She collected her bags and left. It was the end of the day-shift and Elaine's shift was just beginning. Oscar handed her the book she'd been studying the last time he saw her.

"I was just kidding about the sex, didn't mean to be offensive. Take it."

"No."

"Come on."

"I..." Elaine looked around. The locker room had emptied, "I don't want to. Thanks."

He withdrew his hand and turned around.

"You're kind," Elaine said to his back.

Oscar turned back towards her. He held his hands up in the air, puffing out his lips, and feigned exasperation, although it was not all pretense.

"I'm trying here," he said, squeezing his face to signal frustration.

"What is it you want?"

"I want you to have this."

"Is that all?"

"I don't know." He laughed. "Maybe friendship? Contrary to what you might think, I don't have many." He was facing her, smiling. "I could certainly do with some company." He watched her smile.

The austerity of her face, her whole body, lifted. Her lips were full, a pale pink color, and she had a chip in her front tooth.

◦◦

The University teacher was lonelier than Elaine imagined such people could be. It wasn't that she naively thought wealthy or educated people were never lonely. Rather it was his gregariousness that she imagined would have inoculated him against this common human experience. She'd seen him around the department usually in a loud conversation with his colleagues or, if walking alone, calling out to people he passed by. She'd imagined someone like him surrounded by people. But as it turned out, no. Elaine found that she liked him. She liked the way, now she could see it, he used this big personality to hide something more delicate and in need. She liked his loud voice. The way he was preposterous when she said she'd never learned anything about Nigeria in High School. He was big, he filled a room, and she liked that.

◦◦

"I think you're beautiful," Oscar said to Elaine, emboldened by the weeks that had passed and their growing contact.

He leaned back on the giant steps of Rhodes Memorial, putting his arm around her shoulders. They'd taken the steep but short walk up from the university, taking advantage of the few hours before Elaine's evening shift began. They sat, dwarfed by lions and a horse, myths and history hanging over their burgeoning attraction, the shadows of the monument diminishing as the sun disappeared.

"Only half of me," Elaine replied.

SUNDAY 13TH SEPTEMBER 1992

For Lékè:

It was always at the farm. That was where we could speak without my mother's interruption. My dad would collect me from school on his okada and we'd drive fast, cutlass and hoe sticking out of the basket at the back. My mother seldom came with us. She complained the sun blistered her skin and anyway she preferred the coolness of the university library.

But the first time, we were all there together. Touch-me-nots made a low green brush over most of the ground and ran tracks through the soft soil. I frightened the weeds, each feathery leaf closing on the instant of my contact. While my parents walked around speaking of fertilizers and what they would put where, I waited for the folded leaves to open again.

MONDAY 21ST SEPTEMBER 1992

Elaine put her lips to Léke's ear. In two months, he'd grown so much, her arm ached if she held him for too long. His feet were long and bony. He'll be tall, she realized. She settled back into the wooden park bench, arranged the baby so he suckled the way the nurse had shown her.

She'd phoned the Superette earlier.

"Where are you?" asked Ursula. "Haddad's asking."

"Léke has a fever this morning. I'm at the clinic, just waiting to see the day nurse."

"Listen, when you're not here, he hassles me about that, OK?"

"Tell him I'm coming."

"He said you should quit and not cause problems."

"Tell him I'm coming. I need the work." The line was silent. "Ursula? You there?" She'd hung up.

"Mummy, look!" A young boy dangled from the jungle gym with one hand. Elaine guessed he was four, perhaps five.

The mother stood a few meters away, pushing a pram back and forth with one hand. With the other, she smoked a cigarette. She looked furtive, as if any moment someone might catch her and put her in handcuffs. Elaine looked

away, then down at Lékè. He finished suckling and she re-
arranged her clothing, draping him over her shoulder and
rubbing his back. His little head resting against her heart
was burning with the fever.

Across the wide road, in front of the park, was Chapel
Street Clinic. Holding the baby to her chest, Elaine
crossed the road and walked into the dark coolness of the
building. She walked past a young girl pushing a child in a
wheelchair. The girl was crying but the toddler's face was
dry and still, serious, in a way that would scare an adult.
Initially it looked to Elaine, as the girl and the child in the
wheelchair approached, that the child's eye was missing.
As they got closer, it looked more like an accident had
happened. Something terrible. The child caught Elaine's
stare with the one working eye. The other looked ahead,
inflamed and unseeing.

In the waiting area, more women had gathered since
Elaine had arrived an hour ago. She went up to the woman
with the toddler strapped to her back and, with a small
smile, regained her place in the queue. A nurse walked
along the line collecting the Road-to-Health cards. She
came back a few minutes later, a stack of files in the crook
of her arm and a frown on her face. Another nurse appeared
from a room to the side of the waiting hall. Elaine remembered her from her last immunization visit—kind eyes with
a funny habit of wiping her palms against the breast of her
white shirt, as if she'd just washed them. She had a young
face. She started calling out names, doing a triage, and
mothers moved with their babies into the weighing room.
The nurse collecting the cards got to Elaine.

"He's hot," Elaine said. "I need to see someone."

The nurse gave her a sharp look then moved along to
the next woman in the queue.

"I said, he's—"

"Wait, you!" the nurse snapped.

After she'd collected all the cards, she came back to
Elaine. "Has he been immunized? Hmmm?"

"Yes."

"On time?"

"Yes. Yes."

"Name?"

"Lékè." Saying his name made her cry but she covered it up as best she could.

The nurse rifled through the cards, spilling some onto the grey-tiled floor. A mother nearby picked them up and handed them back to her. The nurse retrieved Lékè's from the stack of cards and studied it.

"Come with me," she said and Elaine followed her down a narrow corridor. They turned a corner and the passage widened.

"Wait here." The nurse handed back Lékè's card.

Elaine joined the other waiting mothers, some of whom she recognized from the front room, sent through after their children were weighed. There were no seats left on the bench so she leaned against the wall.

The line moved quickly. There were two nurses seeing to them, each with her own consulting room. Elaine heard her name called and entered the small room.

"Please sit down." It sounded as if the nurse was talking with her hand covering her mouth.

A side window let in a breeze and Elaine shivered. A hard-looking bed with a thin blue cloth thrown over it sat against a wall.

"Morning. Can I see the card please?"

She always kept it safe in the house; maybe if she kept his Road-to-Health card safe, that would make up for all the other things she could not control.

"He's not gaining? Hmmm, what's wrong with Baby, is he drinking? Still on the breast?"

"Yes."

"Is he vomiting? Diarrhea?"

Elaine shook her head.

"Does he feed regularly?"

"Not always. He's hot and he doesn't sleep at night. Sometimes he doesn't take the breast. When I check the blankets, they're wet. With sweat."

"For how long has this been going on?"

They sat, their chairs at an acute angle and Lékè on Elaine's lap.

"A few days?"

"Why did you wait so long?" The nurse asked then her face softened and she shifted her chair closer so she could examine Lékè. "Where do you live, Elaine?"

"Salt River."

"And work?"

"Grocery shop. Cashier."

"Are you alone in the house? Baby's father?"

Elaine shook her head but the nurse wasn't sure which question she was answering. She was about to rephrase the question but stopped when she realized Elaine was crying.

"And food." She pressed on, reaching a hand to Elaine's shoulder. "Are you eating properly?"

Elaine looked down at the floor. She'd been sleeping less and less over the past few nights.

"We can give Baby formula to supplement." The nurse seemed relieved to be able to offer something. "Always try and feed from the breast first though. But we'll give you formula as a last measure. Let me examine. Hold him. Like that."

She leaned forward, blowing onto her hands to warm them. Lékè stayed still as she put the thermometer underneath his arm. After recording the mercury level, she checked his skin for dehydration. She pulled the stethoscope from around her neck and placed it to his chest. Lékè let out a cry—he didn't like the cold instrument against his skin. The nurse moved on with her examination but now he was upset and the crying continued. She used a flat stick to hold his tongue down but his cries pressed through. In fact, it seemed to Elaine that he became indignant. The nurse was unbothered but Elaine winced—despite being sick, he cried so seldom. She could never get used to it.

The nurse checked his ears. She nodded to herself. She warmed her hands again and checked his body for any rashes. She felt his tummy.

"Shh, shh," Elaine calmed Lékè. "Nearly done. Nearly. Nearly," she sang and he was momentarily distracted by the pitch of her voice.

The nurse smiled. She sat back into the chair and scribbled on Lékè's card. "He has a temperature. 39.7 degrees is very high. I'll mix some antibiotics for him." She indicated the trolley alongside her, filled with packets and tubes of medicine.

Elaine regarded it with suspicion.

"His ear is red. Middle-ear infection. Otitis media." She wrote as she talked, looking up with soft eyes every now and then. "And I'm concerned about his weight too, he's failing to thrive. But let's start giving the milk supplement and review within a week. Also some Panado and vitamin syrup."

She returned the pen to the pocket in her navy-blue jacket and handed Elaine the Road-to-Health card. She prepared the antibiotics, taking the pen out again to write the instructions on the packet.

"See you in a week." She rose and Elaine stood too.

"Is he OK, Nurse?"

"He'll be fine. Make sure he feeds. Come back next week," she repeated.

Elaine nodded but even as she did so, she worried about how all this would work out. She knew she could not keep taking days off, Haddad would eventually simply fire her. It would not be right but he had done things before that were not right. People did unright things all the time with no consequence, she knew this, she had lived it.

After leaving the clinic, Elaine walked with Lékè through the streets, heading for home. She felt the thinness of her mind, her thoughts like a million fireflies, bright and sparkling but soon dead. She couldn't keep one line of thought going for long enough to reach clear decisions. For instance, the Haddad problem. And Lékè's sickness. And she must remember to return next week. The medicines. She must remember the medicines. At home, she spread the packets along with the large tin of formula on top of the bed and looked at them for a while.

There was a woman on the street that ran a small crèche but once she heard of Lékè's illness, she cautioned Elaine not to bring him back till he was fully recovered. When Elaine's landlady came home, she begged her to watch Lékè while she went for the night-shift. The woman reluctantly agreed.

Later at work, seated at the checkout counter, Elaine felt a cool wetness on her stomach and looked down. Milk had soaked through her uniform. Panicked, she looked up but the customer was not paying attention. She finished ring-ing up the items, put the money in the till, and completed the transaction.

"Ursula, I need to take a break."

Ursula pulled a face but moved to Elaine's place behind the counter.

Elaine looked at her watch. The landlady had only agreed to watch Lékè for a few hours. Elaine would have to ask permission to end her shift early.

She put on a sweater in the locker room and knocked on the manager's door.

"Yes?"

Elaine walked in, shutting the door behind her. "Mr. Haddad."

"Marriot?" He looked up from a stack of papers on his desk.

She'd worked there for almost eight months—ever since she'd been dismissed from the cleaning agency—but regardless of how long they'd worked for him, Haddad called his employees by their surnames and insisted they do the same with him.

"My baby isn't well."

He stared at her, waiting for her to speak further. His face remained unmoved.

"I'm requesting time off. Please."

He shook his head.

"I need the time off to take care of my baby."

He attempted to remain calm. This seemed to require

that he hiss rather than speak. "Marriot, this isn't Red Cross. If you need help, go to some other place." Flecks of spit dropped on the papers in front of him. "Anything else?"

"I...I need to leave early today. My baby is ill."

He nodded. "We'll dock time off from your week's wages."

As Elaine left his office, he said, "There are many people who want to work, Marriot, even if you do not."

SUNDAY 26TH AUGUST 2012

A squirrel sprang from one chestnut tree to another. It seemed in a hurry. Marcus brushed aside the dried leaves that had settled on Jane's stone. He crouched down and started arranging the flower pots he'd carried from the car.

After the burial, Lékè had insisted they plant Four O'Clocks, although Marcus had never once heard Jane speak about them. He vaguely remembered her derisive feelings towards perennial flowers. As Marcus arranged the flowers, he made uneven whistling sounds. He didn't hear Lékè coming up from behind him.

Lékè cleared his throat. Marcus looked over his shoulder.

He hadn't seen Lékè since the attempted birthday dinner. "You're here," Marcus said.

Lékè nodded in response but the old man didn't see.

Since Lékè had moved out six months before, they'd arranged to see each other every Sunday. Lékè didn't always make it to the cemetery and, after his visit, Marcus would eat lunch alone. The times when Lékè did arrive, Marcus was never sure how he really felt about it—a combination of irritated surprise and disappointment.

"Help me with this," Marcus said.

The two worked on the well-tended gravesite, replaced the wilting flowers with the new ones.

"Work?" Marcus asked to ease his discomfort.

"Fine."

Marcus wanted to bring up the letters again but didn't know how.

Lékè finished patting the soil down around the cutting

he'd just planted. He sat down on the ground next to Jane's tombstone, and looked at the familiar engraved letters: Jane Bisset 1953–2002. Beloved wife and mother.

"How's your place? I should come by," Marcus said, rising from his crouch to look at Lékè now studying the ground in front of him.

They stretched the conversation out as long as it would go, then went to a nearby bistro for Sunday lunch.

Lékè gave Marcus his order and got up to use the bathroom. Marcus waved his hand in the air, trying to get the waiter's attention.

"How's it going, Professor?" the waiter said.

"Ah. Justin, right? Good to see you. Getting a bite to eat with my son." He gestured to the empty chair and the waiter nodded. Marcus smiled, nervous.

His face was sunken and he looked ten years older than his sixty-seven. Finding his hands unsteady and shaking, he'd recently stopped shaving and a rough beard claimed his face. Behind his glasses, his aging eyes watered regularly.

He and Jane used to frequent this place. The name and owners had changed over the years. After they adopted Lékè, but before Jane fell ill, they would come here together, as a family.

"What can I get for you?" the waiter asked.

Marcus remembered how Jane would peer at the menu, turning her wedding band the way she did whenever she was nervous, and no matter how long she stared at the menu, Jane always ordered the roast duck with orange sauce and a glass of sweet white. Both Marcus and Lékè would raise their eyebrows.

"Come on, Jane, try something different," Marcus would say.

She'd brush him aside and, with an earnest look, turn the pages and ask the waiter what specials they had. Finally, she'd say, "Maybe I should just have the duck."

Marcus placed the orders. Two steaks. His well done, and Lékè liked his bloody. The waiter left to get the drinks—

a water and a Coke.

Across the room, behind a glass partition, you could see into the kitchen, see the chef chopping vegetables. A fire crackled in the corner; a large table near the fire warmed with heavy voices and laughter. The roof was low, with elaborate white stucco patterns against the golden glow of the ceiling. Along the floor, the stretch of terracotta tiles was broken intermittently with colorful rugs.

Why did they keep coming back here? Was it some act of devotion to her? Her memory. Was it a pretence? Did he think one day when they walked in, there she'd be waiting for them, her order for duck on the waiter's card, her glass of wine in hand? After she fell ill, all joy was rinsed from life. And left to raise Lékè after her death, it seemed to Marcus an uneven exchange.

◆◆

Lékè leaned back and let his head hit against the wall. He heard someone wash their hands outside the cubicle, the clank of the towel machine and then the door click behind them. He took off his right shoe, fishing from out of the boot a cellophane bag. Inside was the photograph of the small woman in a blue coat. It had seemed like a good hiding place when he'd retrieved the photograph from the bottom of his suitcase in the morning. He'd suddenly wanted it close again.

He never did get to ask Jane who the woman in the picture was. It had felt as though the question had stuck in his mouth, lodged there, and threatened to choke him. Lékè studied the picture. She was looking right at him with piercing large grey eyes. Her pale cheeks were freckled and her short hair cut around her ears. At the back of the photograph was the still indecipherable word. He'd decided it was a name, that seemed sensible. He'd also decided that she was someone important. He stopped short of calling her anything else.

Lékè turned back to the front of the photograph. He looked at a face that had become deeply familiar over the years. In fact sometimes when he looked at the picture, it seemed to him that he knew the woman standing, that they'd spoken one time long ago and that soon enough they'd speak again. He rubbed the face with his index finger. He resented the way Marcus had sprung talk about an envelope on him. An envelope. A packet. A collection of things for him to consider. Things from before.

Despite never giving her the official title, Lékè was ten when he realized who he was looking at.

That night, he had dreamed he was flying over a strange mass he could not recognize from above. It looked like some kind of tangle of dark wires. He imagined it was what his afro looked like if someone looked down on his head. Coaxed by the wind—encouraging him to go everywhere, explore everything, and leave nothing undiscovered—he dove down towards the strange thing. He just kept diving and diving and diving and diving.

"I should be there by now," he said to the wind but there came no reply.

He suddenly realized the air around him had disappeared and he was struggling to breathe. Understanding that he had gone too far, he moved to fly back upwards but something gripped him. He couldn't see them but indeed he had flown into the mass of dark wires. They felt more like sticky roots grabbing at his limbs and body. Making licking sounds, the saliva of this beast like acid on his skin. As he took his last breath, he noticed that the inside of the belly of his captor was pasted with the same photograph he'd kept all these years. He couldn't breathe and she watched him.

After that, more and more nightmares had invaded his dream-life so that, exhausted after a night of struggle, he would fall asleep at his desk at school. He dropped two grades by the end of term exams.

"Is it hard at home?" the young school guidance counselor asked.

The steel chair was cold and soothing against the backs of Lékè's knees.

"We know your mum is seriously ill."

"She's not my mum."

Lékè's nightmares continued. He would wake up sweating and crying and Jane would come to comfort him. "Bad dream?" she'd say, not switching the lights on but coming and settling on the edge of the bed. Her bony hands found the bump of his legs.

She was sick. Dying. But Lékè couldn't help himself. "How did you find me? Did my mother throw me away?" He couldn't see her face but he could hear, in her silence, that he'd asked something true and that now she would find a gentle way to lie to him.

"No, sweetheart."

"Yes, that's what happened."

"No."

But she was slow to make up a story and when it finally came, a hollow was already inside him.

"You...you were precious. You are so precious, Lékè."

"Who gave me my name?"

"Oh..."

He felt sorry for goading her. He realized how unable she was. "I'm sorry, Mummy."

She reached for him and Lékè let himself be hugged.

"You came like an angel, Lékè."

Later in his dreams, he wore black wings like a cape around his neck, for decoration, perhaps because he couldn't fly.

Some of the nightmares still persisted but fewer than before. Jane never came again to comfort him. Instead, she sent Marcus. After she died, no one came.

Over time, the nightmares dimmed but his sleep was never the same again. Sometimes missing that sleeping world of unbounded adventure hurt his heart and he cried when he was by himself.

❧

Lékè placed the photograph back and put on his shoes. Back in the restaurant, the heated air from the fire warmed his face but the conversation with Marcus remained tight and cold.

"How's Red? You fix the wipers yet?"

Lékè nodded, watched as Marcus drained his wine glass.

Marcus signaled to the waiter. "Want some dessert, Lékè?"

The ice-cream shocked Lékè's teeth. The pain was too much and he left his bowl half full. Marcus finished his, the chink of the spoon on the bowl joining the chorus of other eating noises in the restaurant.

"See you next week?" Marcus asked, digging his hands into his pockets, jingling his car keys and scanning the parking lot for his car. Lékè nodded, but Marcus wasn't looking. Having spotted his car, he turned to Lékè and tried to hug him. Lékè tightened, and Marcus patted his shoulder instead. "Take care, son."

❧❧

Lékè walked towards home, ignoring taxi drivers hooting and calling for him to jump in. He counted his footsteps in groups of one hundred, starting again after each century. A pair of lovers held hands and kissed in the corner of a bus shelter. In the verge, a homeless man jerked off underneath a tattered blanket. Another ragged woman cursed her husband who walked behind her, pushing an empty trolley and cursing her back.

He saw a large sign advertising a funeral parlor.

The morning of Jane's funeral, the house was full of people. Jane was popular at the high school she'd taught at before she fell ill and Marcus had a big family. Between Jane's sister and her family, Marcus's five older sisters, their families and a bunch of school kids in uniform, Lékè didn't recognize his own home. He hadn't known where to sit.

They drove to the church in a long skinny black car. It gleamed and Lékè liked it when he stood beside the car and saw his curved reflection.

At the church, the family was led in and seated. The large hall filled up with people, most of whom Lékè didn't recognize.

Jane was to be cremated. After everyone was seated,

Marcus and four of the matric students walked alongside the hearse. She was sleeping, not moving at all. And she was wearing a white dress, with puffy sleeves, that Lékè had never seen.

Later, when Lékè asked Marcus what his mother was wearing, Marcus explained that Jane had asked to be buried in her wedding dress.

"Why?"

"I don't know, my boy."

They sat on a bench in the garden, hiding from the guests eating and drinking in the house. The garden had once been photographed by *House & Garden*. Jane had won best letter of the month and part of the prize was a garden makeover and photos in the following month's issue.

Further along Main Road, Lékè noticed people carrying familiar shopping bags. He'd already spent the morning in the mall but after the lunch with Marcus, he didn't want to go back home just yet.

The Plaza Mall closed its doors at 10 pm every night except Friday and Saturday nights when it stayed open an hour longer.

Lékè waited at the entrance. A woman in a peak cap and tennis shoes, tall but dressed simply in tracksuit pants and T-shirt. He followed her into the mall.

She headed straight for the supermarket. In aisle 2, a shop attendant was stacking Cornflakes next to Rice Crispies. The woman lingered, appraising the cereals. Lékè used the attendant as a cover and tried to catch a better look at the woman—she had on dark glasses which barely concealed a bruised cheek and black eye. When she left the aisle, Lékè followed. She filled two baskets—frozen peas, canned goods, cleaning products, cereals—and joined the queue to check out. As she wandered out the supermarket and back into the mall, her cellphone rang. "Yes?" she shouted. "What is it? ... I'm on my way... Yah, well, fuck you too! Fuck you! I hate you... I said I'm on my way, for God's sake!" She shoved the phone into her bag and some internal seal seemed to break. She flung her head back and cursed some more, screaming into the hollow insides of the mall. The moment passed and, pinned by the stares of other mall-goers, she walked out towards the car park, sniveling.

Beside her car, her hands full, she looked around for someone to help her open the door. Lékè, walking past, obliged.

"Thank you so much," she said after she'd piled the bags into the back of the car. "So kind," she continued, her voice muffled as she tried to hide her face with her hand. Lékè nodded in response and backed away.

Later that night, he lay awake in bed; he'd wanted something to remember her by but hadn't been able to take anything fast enough.

His sleep was disturbed by a recurring dream in which he was standing in a deep hole. Above his head he could hear the sound of digging and every few seconds soil rained down on him.

"Who are you?" he shouted.

"It's me," his voice called back at him.

MONDAY 27TH AUGUST 2012

Lékè nodded in Lewis's direction as he clocked in. The security guard, sitting on a chair by the door, pursed his lips in response—Lékè was ten minutes late. The workers who were friendly with Lewis would go to lunch without clocking out and he would look away while they were leaving, as if he didn't notice. But with Lékè, Lewis was always watching. Lékè was certain it was Lewis who'd lodged the hygiene complaint against him. He looked back to see Lewis scowl as he climbed up the steps.

A dark corridor, with the manager's office to the left, led into an open plan space. Lékè walked past the auditors and went to his cubicle. There was no natural light on his side of the office, but a pot plant with spiky green leaves and placed on the worn carpet endured nonetheless, surviving on the half-finished cups of rooibos tea that he emptied into its soil. Lékè sat down at his desk without removing his backpack, and turned on his computer.

"Hey, Lékè!"

Gene had joined the company five days before, and was still unaware of the hidden rule among the staff: ignore Lékè.

Lékè tilted his head to acknowledge his new neighbor.

Gene was half distracted, adjusting the height of his monitor. He'd been doing this since he'd arrived, complaining to Lékè over his shoulder that "They don't make things for tall people like you and me, pal."

"How was your weekend?" Gene asked, stretching up and smoothing his hands over his brush-cut auburn hair.

Gene's face, less pale than his hands, was tanned a light bronze.

"OK," Lékè said.

"Do anything interesting? Did you catch that movie with the hot chick on SABC 1? With the–" He cupped his hands in front of his chest.

"No."

Someone sniggered and Gene looked around the office, confused. He shrugged, asked, "You watch the rugby?"

"No," Lékè said, as he punched in his computer password.

Gene sighed and turned back to his computer.

At 12:15 pm, Lékè got up. The talk in the tea pause area quietened as he dropped a teabag into his mug. At his desk he took off his backpack and pulled out a cellophane bag with five rusks in it. He ate one, careful to collect the crumbs that fell on the desk and wipe them into the dustbin—the cleaner had complained about the bits of food and the cockroaches they'd attracted.

Immediately after finishing his first cup of tea, Lékè got up to make himself a second.

Back at his desk again, Gene had wheeled his chair out between the desk clusters and was gawking at something. Lékè looked to see what he was staring at.

Two women chatted a few desks up. One, tall, stood leaning forward, her hands spread on the desk. The other sat holding a leaflet the tall one had handed to her. She

scanned it and asked something. The tall one pointed towards a side wing where the board room was located. After
a few seconds the woman sitting down shook her head and
returned the flyer.

The tall woman walked on, stopping at each desk till
finally she got to where Lékè and Gene sat.

"Hey, sweetheart." Gene dropped his voice a tone
lower.

"Hi. I'm Tsotso."

"Gene. He's Lékè." He took her hand and she had to
prize it back from him.

"Not sure if you guys saw the posters. I arranged with
WPBC to have a blood clinic here. It's today. Will you come
through and donate?"

"I will if you're inviting me."

She didn't smile. She handed them each a flyer and
waited while they skimmed through it. "GIVE BLOOD," it
said, in bold lettering.

"You do this often?" Gene put the flyer aside, leaned
back in his chair, and stared at her.

"I spend a lot of time in hospitals, around nurses. I guess
their lectures on blood donation finally got to me." She was
very matter-of-fact.

"How'd you get Robocop in on it? Boss man doesn't
even know we exist." He leaned forward on his chair. "You
must have special powers."

Tsotso frowned and looked towards Lékè who had
turned back to his computer. "Are you coming?"

"Yeah yeah yeah, we're coming," Gene said.

She looked back at Gene and then Lékè. "OK, starts at
midday. Bring your IDs."

Gene watched her walk on to the next desk. "Nice," he
said. "Very, very nice."

◆◆

A line formed. It wound through the office and ended at
the boardroom door. Lékè and Gene joined the queue. They
looked out for Tsotso but didn't see her. Every ten minutes
or so the boardroom door was opened and, craning his

neck, Lékè caught a glimpse of the action inside.

"Nervous?" Gene asked. "I hate needles, by the way. I hate blood. Can't stand the prick of the needle. That's what I can't take. And they make you watch, you know? You nervous?"

Lékè scuffed his shoe into the carpet.

"You think she'll be hot? The nurse?" Gene strained to see how fast the line was moving. "That's one of the reasons I'm doing this," he smirked.

Lékè wiped his palms on his chest; he usually did his best to avoid hospitals and clinics.

Gene noticed a colleague butting into the queue. "Hey. Join from the back, man! Some of us have been waiting a while."

Gene went in before Lékè and then the door opened and it was finally Lékè's turn. Inside, there were three desks and three beds set up.

The nurse at one of the desks wore no lipstick and the flesh around the tips of her nails was raw and reddened. "Please sit down. Could you fill this in? It's a lifestyle survey which is mandatory for all donors."

Lékè took long to fill in the form.

"Have you had sexual activity with a male or female prostitute, escort or sex worker, or exchanged money, drugs, goods or favors in return for sex?"

He hesitated. Nothing had happened that night though, he thought, remembering the woman's caked make-up and wobbly high heels. The look on her face when he'd told her he'd changed his mind.

"Finished?" the nurse asked.

Lékè signed his name and handed her the form. She glanced over it before adding it to a pile. "Thanks. Have you donated before?"

"Blood?"

She smiled. "Yes, what else?"

Lékè shook his head.

"OK. Let's register you. Your ID, please. Thanks. I'll issue you with a card. Next time you donate, you can use it as identification." She handed Lékè the card. "Next I need to do a finger prick test, just checking your iron levels. Give me your right hand please."

Her hand felt soft, pudgy. Lékè winced at the pin prick.

She left for a short while then returned. "OK, come lie on the bed. Let's check your pressure and pulse."

Everything was fine.

"OK. Your arm please. Other arm. Thanks." She had a young face but her ample figure lent her a maturity, a kind of confidence—she didn't seem to mind that she took up space.

A silver nametag on the breast of her white uniform said Adielah Moses. Her neck sat in rolls of cream-colored flesh beneath her chin. She wore horseshoe earrings and fine dark hair grew along the sides of her face, other strands of hair escaping from the flowered scarf pinned around her head.

"Place your arm here, to the side."

Lékè did as she asked.

She tied a light grey strap around his bicep. The scratch of the strap was rough, in contrast to her clammy palms against his skin. The pressure from her touch excited him. He worried that she would notice.

"I've never done this before," he blurted out as she dabbed his arm with cool cotton wool.

She smiled. With her other hand, she reached for the needle and a collection bag. "This might hurt," she said but, as she pierced his skin, what Lékè felt was strangely pleasant. He thought of Red first, then Jane, and his hand jerked.

The nurse noticed. "Try to keep still please," she said, keeping her eyes on the vial.

He answered with a sigh, watching as the blood pooled in the plastic collection bag. At the sight of the bright burgundy, his body prickled and his head filled with air. His mind drifted. He remembered putting his ear to Jane's stomach and hearing all the noises of her insides. She'd laughed at him. That was the day he'd learned the word "stethoscope." Some days later, in Dr. Naidoo's examination room, he learned its function.

"Finished, all done. Just apply some pressure there for me."

Lékè put his hand on the cotton wool while Adielah applied a thin strip of gauze to hold it in place. He felt heavy again and disappointment came over him like the shadow of a rain cloud.

"Is that it?" he heard himself say.

"Quick, nuh? Easy peasy."

He lifted into a sitting position. On rising, he felt faint and grabbed hold of the nurse for support.

"Hey! Careful," she said. "Sit there for awhile. I'll bring you some juice and biscuits. Keep drinking throughout the day, and eat a good meal. Try not to do anything too strenuous."

"Thank you," Lékè said, surprised to find himself missing the sensation of her skin on his.

While Adielah arranged some biscuits and a polystyrene cup of juice onto a tray, Lékè stayed sitting and looked around the room at the other two stations; still feeling dazed, he closed his eyes for thirty seconds. When he opened them, Tsotso was standing over him. Her skin was dark, a deep brown color, and she had a darker mole, the size of a guava seed, just beneath her left eye. Without it, Lékè thought, she would not have been beautiful.

"You all right?"

Lékè's tongue had stuck to the bottom of his mouth.

"What are you—mute? Or is it 'cuz your wing man isn't here?" She stared for a few seconds, unforgiving, and left.

Shaken, Lékè ate the biscuits on offer and wandered out of the makeshift blood clinic. He found Gene at his desk, almost blue in the face, his eyes wide, but within a few minutes, his color came back. Every few minutes, he threw a comment at Lékè over his shoulder.

"That nurse, hey? What do you say, freaking amateur. She couldn't find my vein—stuck holes in me like a bloody pincushion. How was yours?"

Lékè didn't reply.

After another few minutes, "Psst."

Lékè turned around to look at Gene, indicating with a crooked finger for Lékè to come closer. The woman working in the adjoining cubicle turned too. Lékè got up. He'd been unable to do any work since returning from the clinic, distracted by the memory of Tsotso's face staring at him.

Gene grabbed Lékè's inner-arm where the gauze protected the puncture.

"My girlfriend's at home today," Gene said, raising his eyebrows as though checking that Lékè understood the unspoken significance of this. He winked then waited a few seconds before continuing.

"Come here." He waved his hand, signaling for Lékè to bend down so Gene could whisper. His breath was damp. It came out hot, but cooled quickly, leaving a chilling sensation along Lékè's jaw line and the side of his neck.

From the day Gene arrived, Lékè had been taken aback by his friendliness, overwhelmed at times. A part of him wanted Gene to leave him alone but another part, more unfamiliar, enjoyed the contact and the attention.

Lékè listened as Gene spoke. The idea was not without faults. It was the kind of plan that would work once, but never more than that.

"What do you think?" Gene asked, grinning into Lékè's face.

Lékè thought for a few seconds then nodded. He'd spent several afternoons dreaming of ways to leave the office so that he could disappear into the hustle of the Plaza Mall. Just over half way through the year and he'd already used up all his sick leave.

"Is that a yes? You in? OK, here goes."

Lékè discovered that Gene, while not a great performer, had the gift of deception. Gene feigned collapse at the water dispenser. Later on, he complained to Lékè that he had banged his head for real and was going to sue the company for damages. In the moment, despite his apparent delicate state, Gene managed to explain to his colleagues how he shouldn't have given blood, and how he needed to leave work immediately and rest at home.

"Lékè can take me. I can't drive my car like this," Gene shouted out before anyone else could volunteer.

Lékè stepped forward from the crowd. His license had expired but he thought it best not to mention that. Gene maintained a veneer of hysteria but Lékè doubted it was sufficient enough to stop people from wondering whether the thing was a hoax. Regardless, his act succeeded in fending off anyone from actually saying anything. Lékè gathered their belongings and they were both out the door, under the suspicious glare of Lewis.

"We did it," Gene said as they neared his car. "Look, you can be on your way. I've got business to attend to."

Lékè watched Gene's wiry frame settle in front of the steering wheel of his car and whiz away. The fumes from the old Ford made him cough. He started walking. His feet knew where to carry him, hungry for whatever the mall would offer.

Within minutes of arriving at Plaza Mall, Lékè spotted, from the throng of old people and housewives, a short woman walking with a black sack slung round her shoulder. Her hair was a bush of grey locks. She was elderly but walked in firm confident strides. She barked requests at the shop attendants when she couldn't find what she wanted.

Lékè followed her into the chemist.

She looked up to a high shelf then looked around. Seeing Lékè, she said, "Young man, you're nice and tall. Could you help me get that blue bottle there? With the white cap."

Lékè walked towards her, unsure whether to smile or look serious. He reached it easily and handed her the bottle.

"Thank you. These days, I need to go shopping with my granddaughter. She's taller than me and the shelves are so high. Back when she was little, I was the one getting things off the top shelf." She giggled. "Times change on you."

Lékè nodded as if he understood and moved away.

"Thanks again," the woman called after him.

He stood outside the chemist some distance from the entrance and when she came out, he followed her. When she exited through the back of the mall, Lékè kept up behind her all the way to the bus stop. She waited for a few minutes and then suddenly became frantic. She searched through her bag, looking for something. She took the bag off her shoulder and placed it on the ground. She bent over and started swearing to herself. She'd lost something, something important. He watched as she searched her body. He knew what she was looking for. It was something small enough to fit between the pages of a book. Despite being frenzied, she managed to be delicate with the front and back of a deep blue leather-covered Gideon Bible. She held up the dainty covers and dangled the pages. Nothing. She took out the smallest purse Lékè had ever seen. Nothing. She checked if it wasn't underneath her bra strap. And then she looked in all the places she'd already looked. Lékè, following, watched as, hassled, she turned back to the mall and reported her loss to the security guard who nodded but couldn't help her. Back again at the bus-stop, she started to cry; her face crumpled, revealing years of wear.

Lékè thought he would tap her on her shoulder and say, "Ma'am, you seem to have dropped these. Here you go."

The Golden Arrow bus pulled off Main Road and the old woman got on, still crying. Lékè watched the bus go.

At home, he put the earrings under his pillow. He'd seen her buy them after she'd been to the chemist and then watched them drop out of her bag when she'd passed clothes over the counter at the dry cleaners. Shiny studs that twinkled in the weak winter sunlight. Maybe they were for her granddaughter. Imagining the earrings on Tsotso, he squeezed each piece of jewelry between his thumb and index finger; the gold stems left a mark.

◆◆

Some days after his first experience of giving blood, while on his way to work, Lékè noticed posters in a shop window encouraging blood donors.

"I'd like to donate," he said, walking in and addressing the man sitting at the desk.

"Good day, sir. Have you given blood before?"

"Uh, yes."

"When was the last time you gave blood, sir?"

"Three days ago."

"Oh, I'm sorry, sir, but you can only give blood every fifty-six days. Would you like to fill out this form, then when you come back, we'll already have you on our records?"

Crestfallen, Lékè sat down to fill in the form. At the top of the form was a list of tests that were available.

"Can I have my blood pressure measured?" Lékè asked.

The man looked up from his work. "Yes. The nurse comes in on Mondays and Wednesdays for all those tests. I'm just assisting with admin." He bobbed his head in apology.

"And the annual check-up?"

"Sir, you'd need to go to the City Hospital for that. Here's a card with the address."

❧

The City Hospital sat, a massive obtrusion, among the intricate network of streets in the city center. A knot in a delicate shawl, bright pink with over-sized mouldings, it was an ugly building. Lékè walked past the boom and, following the gate attendant's directions, entered through a small door. He had gone out to lunch, hoping to be done fast enough to claim some minor excuse. He walked through the metal detector which protested with a strident ring. The guard checked Lékè, patting him down along his arms, his torso, and in between his legs. A bulge of coins jingled in Lékè's pocket. Satisfied, the guard let him through.

"Where's the reception, please?"

"Go left here and follow on till after the brown floor. Then turn left again and go straight down. You'll see a sign saying 'Trauma Unit.'"

"Thanks."

Inside the hospital, the passageways were miniature versions of the streets outside, a tapestry of corridors that led nowhere, padlocked rooms. Lékè walked past elevators with heavy doors that vibrated when they opened and closed. The ground was wide grey vinyl flooring with flecks of white. Along one of the walls, there were small square paintings of strange surreal landscapes and austere portraits with names that meant nothing to Lékè etched in brass along the bottoms of the frames. A baby cried out somewhere. Lékè got lost. He spent fifteen minutes wandering through the innards of the hospital. Peeling signs, faded a dull orange, appeared along the corridors, directing to offices and rooms that had died a decade ago. Lékè eventually arrived at the reception, opposite the Trauma Unit, and walked to the main desk.

"I need an appointment with the doctor please. I'm in a rush."

The receptionist didn't look up but pushed forward a clipboard.

"Fill in," he said, still not looking up.

Lékè filled in the form at the desk. There were ten other people waiting. Lékè noticed a father with a little girl asleep in his lap and an old man with a cane, coughing into the already cloistered air of the small room.

"You need to join the queue," the receptionist said to Lékè when he handed back the form.

He was irritated but he found a chair to sit in. Hours passed before the receptionist addressed him.

"Mr. Bisset? This way, please."

Dr. Tembu was small and dark with a greying moustache. He sat behind a desk in a wooden chair and removed his glasses to wipe his eyes as Lékè entered. His hands were large; they belonged to a different body. He beckoned for Lékè to take a seat. "Afternoon. What can I do for you?"

The walls of the room gave Lékè a feeling of being closed in. As he spoke, he kept looking around for a window. The air was stale and the walls were bare.

Dr. Tembu moved around the desk to begin a physical examination. His touch was startling. "Breathe in."

Lékè inhaled.

"And out. Again."

Lékè inhaled.

"Again."

Lékè inhaled. Dr. Tembu's forearm brushed over his chest as he moved the stethoscope from point to point. Lékè's skin tingled.

"Again."

Lékè inhaled. His collar was unbuttoned.

"OK." The doctor hung the stethoscope back around his neck and pulled the thermometer from Lékè's mouth. "Temperature's normal. Just want to check your ears."

Dr. Tembu held Lékè's face and he allowed his head to drop under the gentle pressure of the doctor's fingers. Using an instrument that looked like a metal hammer, the doctor studied first one ear and then the other.

"What's that?" Lékè asked.

"It's an otoscope. With the light and a low-power magnifying glass, I can detect any irregularity." A raised eyebrow suggested amusement. "Have a look."

The instrument was heavier than Lékè imagined. He looked it over and handed it back.

"Everything's fine. Do you have a very stressful job?" Dr. Tembu asked as he walked back to his seat and Lékè buttoned his shirt.

"Not really."

"Well." The doctor smiled, kindly. "I suggest a basic multivitamin. Perhaps some rest. You're a healthy man."

Lékè cleared his throat. "Can I get a flu jab though?"

Gene had mentioned this to him when he was plotting another scam to leave work early.

"Oh?"

"Yes. Just to be safe."

"All right. Let's do that. Come with me."

❧

Lékè moved, stunned, through the streets. He'd thought he would be able to go back to work but it was already half past four. He felt brazen. Lewis and his clock-in can fall off a bridge and die. Lékè walked towards home, too dazed to fully register the old man pissing onto a wall and a beggar with a baby on her back. His footsteps were so leaden, he appeared to be performing a march, solemn and deliberate. Clunk. Clunk. A boy, walking past with his mother, turned around to look. Clunk.

Lékè's head started spinning and he leaned against the wall of a nearby building.

"You OK?" someone asked but he waved him off.

He let the building wall carry him as he tried to untangle his confusion, his experience of being in one of his childhood dreams, the intense euphoria, except this time he was awake. He put his hand to his throat but it was only in his imagination that there was an irritation.

The swirling sensation reduced and Lékè found he could stand proud of the wall without falling.

He passed Elias's shop and stood for a while staring, out of sight, at him and his dog sitting outside on the grubby sidewalk. Whitie was on a chain, and subdued. She licked Elias's ear and he moaned in response.

"Hey, Lékè!" Elias shouted from across the road. "What you buying today? More Four O'Clocks?"

Lékè shook his head and carried on walking. By the time he entered through his gate, the hex from his appointment had worn off. Lewis was real again, alive and menacing. Lékè tried to think of an excuse that would satisfy his manager (stick it to the Clock-In Man) but nothing came to mind. His hands shook as he made himself a cup of tea and for the first time, Lékè noticed loneliness. It swelled into the small space of the studio, a polite and silent guest.

Darkness came. Inside his studio, Lékè tried to sleep but could only manage short bouts. Dr. Tembu and his sandpaper hands; Tsotso's eyes sizing him up; Whitie licking Elias's ear. All of this kept him awake.

He'd never liked animals. Two years after Jane died, when Lékè was twelve, Marcus had bought him a rabbit but he wouldn't touch it, the soft hair, the feel of the muscles moving underneath the thick white fur. After several attempts to place the bunny in Lékè's arms and Lékè refusing, Marcus gave up. Lékè never forgot the squirm of the rabbit's paws in his groin as Marcus had laid the creature in his lap.

Just before he knew he would need to bathe and dress for work, Lékè got out of bed and lay in the back seat of his car. It was cold but he didn't bring his blanket. In the dim light from the street lamp outside, he watched the goose-pimples appear along his arm and blew, checking to see if his breath could warm his skin enough so that the bumps disappeared—an old game from childhood.

THURSDAY 17TH SEPTEMBER 1992

For Lékè:

I have to start with my grandmother, Mama Wōlé. Your great-grandmother. I could go further back but if I'm telling you this story, I must at least start with her.

After a year of marriage to my grandfather—they called him Ògá—her stomach expanded and her dark brown skin gleamed as if she'd rubbed cocoa butter on it.

That was their first son. Wōlé. He was cause for joy, of course. What did they know about the things that lay ahead? They celebrated. Palm-wine. Fish head pepper soup. Iyan.

Nothing scares me, Lékè.

It must be true—the darkness—because nothing scares me. My father was the same. When you get born into a family curse, nothing is frightening. I suppose it's like being the child of an undertaker—dead bodies are commonplace.

I never met Uncle Wōlé or any of my father's brothers. There were six of them, my father being the seventh child.

And then there was an eighth, a girl. That was the beginning of it.

I liked to sit on my haunches and inspect the ground for earthworms. I would split the worms in two with my hoe. I thought because they still wriggled after I split them that it wasn't a bad thing.

"Kai!" my father would shout. "You're killing my farm. Kuro n be. Move, jó! Haba!"

Despite my mother's warnings, my father would tell

me things. "Have I told you yet," he'd begin, "that nothing good will come of us?"

We would settle down, me with an agbalumo fruit or a packet of Orkin biscuits if I was lucky. It would be late afternoon and if I pricked my ears, I could hear cars driving past from town towards the campus we lived on. I would sit beside him on the ground, caught in the crook of his arm, my back pressed against his chest. The same arm held a beer bottle. I reasoned that its content was the cause of our swerving, the jerky journey back home on his motorbike. .

WEDNESDAY 29TH AUGUST 2012

For Tsotso, Western Medical Fund was a stop-gap. Something she could do before opening her workshop and really taking off. She'd taught herself to make violins, with the help of a book she'd downloaded off the Internet and a Chinese man she'd met in a chat room. The notes from the string instrument-making course she'd taken last year helped too.

On the way to work every morning, she stopped in front of Frankie's and stared at the upright piano—a simple "Squire," cherry-wood body. She'd priced it a few months back and had been salivating ever since.

Watching the piano, especially the stool placed in front, reminded Tsotso of her piano lessons in primary school— Mrs. Hendricks sitting next to her, straight-backed, tapping a ruler on her lap and counting along with the metronome. Tsotso always thought but knew better than to ask. It was just one of those things.

Mrs. Hendricks counted out loud. Tsotso counted in her mind, imagining that, somehow or other, the piano counted with them.

As far as Tsotso was concerned, musical instruments had always breathed and lived and spoken; she liked to think she had a special love affair with them, ever since she was five and her uncle had handed her a rusty mbira. She'd held the rough wooden body of the Zimbabwean musical instrument in her small hands and plucked at the row of long slender metal teeth. That was the beginning of the love affair. An affair that had crescendoed, years later, in a boarding school scandal—Tsotso was found lying naked, in the Cecil Skotnes assembly hall, atop the baby grand.

Her academic scholarship at the prestigious school hung in the balance for a few days. Finally, convinced it was part of a Grade 11 prank, the disciplinary committee suspended her for a week and requested, on her return, she make an apology to Mrs. Vuyisiwe, the principal.

Tsotso had borne her punishment, accustomed, by then, to being misunderstood. She hadn't been trying to defile school property, as the teachers suggested. Instead, it was an innocent experiment—she'd wanted to know what it would feel like to have her naked skin pressed up against the skin of the piano. Glorious.

THURSDAY 30TH AUGUST 2012

The smell of her invaded his senses. For several seconds, Léke stood motionless, back against the railing. She moved along the short mall from one shop window to another. He couldn't see her face. She was skinny from behind and her leather handbag hit against her thigh as she walked. She moved on to the next window and Léke followed as close as he could. There was a bench. He sat and, from there, watched her stare into three more stores. When she went along and took the escalators towards the exit, he followed.

It was getting dark outside. It seemed the mall was designed to defy time. Whole days disappeared in the pursuit of objects. The girl was walking fast. Did she know he was behind her? He quickened his pace. Even through the smell of damp tar, her scent still carried. He could almost see it. She turned down a road and he followed. What would he do when he caught up with her? He was still wondering this when she turned around.

"What do you want?"

Léke didn't wait to study her face but turned on his heels. He didn't stop running until he was huddled over catching his breath in Widow Marais's garden.

◦◦

The next day, Lékè left work early. Ignoring Lewis's accusing stare, he walked out of the Western building and headed straight for Plaza Mall. For some months now, a building site opposite the mall had sat shrouded. Clever taglines ran along expensive billboards. From the images it promised some combination of living—Eat Play Work Sleep, it said, introducing the words as if they'd never existed before. Today the shroud was off. Lékè took in the new building and its accompanying multi-tiered parking lot. In fact this had not been the only building site in the neighborhood. Just the week before, Plaza Mall opened its final wing. "Diamond Walk," the sign boards had announced in sequined lettering.

The stores along Diamond Walk were leased out to the most glamorous of retailers. Lékè didn't recognize any of the names but, from the excitement on people's faces and the awe with which they moved from store to store, he gathered the designers were famous. A few of the stores were still vacant, their shop windows boarded up with posters, apologizing for construction and promising luxury in return for patience.

In the stores that had opened their doors, bright clothing hung off the marble-like bodies of mannequins. In the center of this new wing, fitted glass panels high above let the light in but it was no competition for the glare of Diamond Walk. All the surfaces reflected Lékè back to himself, sometimes clearly, sometimes distorted.

He hadn't realized what he was waiting for until he noticed a young girl walking. She looked like she was school-going age although she was not in uniform. On a Friday, the mall would usually start filling with teenagers from around 5 pm. They first changed out of their uniforms in the toilets, commandeered the entrance to the McDonalds outlet and, once it got dark outside, found a corner to neck. Security had a field day trying to keep them in check. Often enough, a parent would be summoned. This girl was ahead of the crowd—it was only just past three o'clock.

She sat down on a bench and Lékè was just about to join her when someone grabbed his arm.

"You, sir!" It was a security guard.

"Excuse me?"

"No loitering in the mall."

"I don't understand."

The guard signaled to a camera hanging from the ceiling. "We've spotted you a couple of times and received complaints. Yesterday a woman reported you chased her." The guard still held Lékè's arm and was leading him towards the back exit. "You may not loiter in the mall, it's a disturbance to our customers."

Apart from the firm grip, there was nothing violent about the encounter. The guard, dressed in a black long-sleeve shirt with a nametag and black trousers, spoke in a low steady tone, diplomatic.

At the exit, he let go of Lékè's arm and left him outside the glass door. Before turning, he pointed to the cameras at the entrance, a silent gesture to say, "We're watching."

Lékè couldn't sleep. His head ached.

At 2 am, he left the studio. Perhaps a walk would tire him out. He avoided the mall area although the crowds would have left by now, the quietly menacing security guard would have gone home surely, and the doors would be locked. Lékè walked towards the new building. Eat Play Work No Sleep, he thought. He smiled. There was still some rubble along the back and bundles of what looked like homeless people sleeping beneath blankets. Lékè walked around the new parking block. At the entrance, the security check was empty.

At 4 am, back home, Lékè drifted into a shallow sleep. He dreamed that he found a little girl living in his roof, in between the rafters; she came down to visit, held his cheeks in her hands, and kissed his face. Her breath on the tip of his nose. He cried in his dream and when he woke, his face was wet. He looked for the girl, looked all around him. But there was no trace of any living thing.

SATURDAY 19TH SEPTEMBER 1992

The ladies from the grocery came by.

"He's a looker, Elaine. He'll break hearts, this one."

All the gossip forgotten, they clucked over him. Elaine was used to not fussing. She felt bad but she often simply left Lékè alone. He was so easy to leave be. He slept, he was content.

"You're not sleeping. At least, you don't look like you are. Is he keeping you up?" Ursula sounded concerned which surprised Elaine.

"Actually he sleeps. But you know, even when he's awake, he waits."

"Waits?"

"Yes. And when he's hungry, if I'm not there he...he doesn't cry, instead he...calls to me."

"Calls to you? What are you talking about?"

Elaine shook her head.

They'd stayed long. Elaine felt ashamed, she hoped they'd be gone before her landlady returned. At least the flat was clean.

Dear Oscar

I'm sorry, I know it's been over a month since I wrote to you.

❦❦

Elaine put the pen down. Her whole body ached and, open or closed, her eyes stung. She hadn't slept all night; her mind wouldn't settle. As soon as it was 7 am, she'd call Ursula and tell her she was ill, not coming in, Bashir would have to cope. She picked up the pen again. She'd already started the letter several times but had not been able to complete it. What could she tell him? She was tired. Something was coming undone.

❦❦

I'm fine. Lékè is growing fast and I whisper your name in his ear every night so he'll know who you are when he meets you. I don't have any photographs of you or I would put them up above where he sleeps.

❦❦

The baby made a noise and she left the unfinshed letter
to check on him. She lifted him and studied his face. When
he was first born, each time she looked at him, she saw her
face and Oscar's eyes. Now, almost two months on, he'd
grown into himself, into his own eyes, and his own expression. She cradled him in her arms. After the first one and
half months of doing poorly, his cheeks had filled out.

Back at the desk, Elaine stared at the letter. After several
minutes, she heard Lékè snoring. She picked up the pen.

◦◦

We miss you, Oscar. Love, Elaine

◦◦

Oscar put away the letter. He hid all of Elaine's letters
inside his pillow. The first time he did it, it had seemed
stupid (something you see on television) but the hiding
place seemed to work. All her letters were there, intact.
Sometimes at night he reached for them, just to feel the
paper.

◦◦

Dear Elaine,
I miss you too and I can't help noticing that your letters
are getting shorter and shorter. Are you OK? Is it Lékè? You
would tell me if there was something wrong, wouldn't you?

Something has happened to me. It is a strange thing—I
don't know if I can explain it to you. I don't want to frighten
you. It's only that...I feel different. And then each time I
receive a shorter and shorter letter from you, I feel even
more different. Until I think one day I'll wake up and I won't
be here anymore.

Oscar felt something crowding him. Over several days,
it had been coming. The letters to Lékè took on a stron-
ger urgency, as if his very intent to tell his son stories was
threatened. He had to write the letters, and guard them,
even from himself.

◦◦

For Lékè:
By the time my grandmother gave birth to her fourth
son, her hair, turned a dull grey, was the texture of straw

and it was falling out. Her skin was caked with a strange rash that disappeared and returned intermittently, chasing itself over different parts of her body. If it left her forehead, it appeared on her breasts and chest. When it left there, it came to the palms of her hands and soles of her feet. She wept as she held Uncle Tuesday in her arms, and begged my grandfather to go with her to the Babaláwo. "Was that the beginning?" I asked my father. I meant the beginning of everything else that came afterwards, of a spell of bad times, Lékè, which is what I am trying to tell you about here.

"No," my father said. "They had been to the Babaláwo before." It was an everyday act, completely normal.

SATURDAY 22ND SEPTEMBER 2012

At 5 pm, Lékè stood in his garden. Since being evicted from the mall, he'd felt flat and listless. He shifted his gaze from the multi-colored flowers to his watch and then back to the soil. The Four O'Clocks remained closed. He leaned over them, intent on nudging them awake. He decided it was the weather's fault, warm for September.

Lékè went back into his studio and lay on the mattress. Maybe the mall would have thinned out. He found himself walking there in his mind, walking into the coolness, his face reflected off the shiny surfaces. The people. The women. He missed it. In fact, his body ached. And so, the other day, he'd done something he'd never done in his young adult life, he'd gone to see a physiotherapist.

"Where does it hurt?"

He was a tall man. Capable looking, with long fingers and dusty-colored hair. He was used to people doing as he asked; Lékè got the feeling no one ever said no to this man. When Lékè had made the appointment, he hadn't known what to expect, he'd never been to a physiotherapist. Now, in answer to the physio's question, Lékè pointed to just below his hairline at the back of his head and flapped his hands to indicate "everywhere."

The physio worked on his neck and back. At one point, he held Lékè's head, his fingers along Lékè's cheeks and his thumbs just beneath his jaw, turning it left and then right. Lékè looked straight ahead, only once darting his eyes sideways to catch a glimpse of a beard revealing shoots of brown hair.

The physiotherapist pressed down at the base of his neck. "Pain?"

"It's OK."

They sat almost folded into one another, the imposing build of the therapist covering most of his patient's body as he worked the knots out of Lékè's neck and shoulders. When the physiotherapist patted him on the shoulder and said, "All done," it seemed to Lékè that no time had passed at all.

The physio stood up and scratched in his cupboard. He talked to Lékè over his shoulder. "Don't use the ointment right away. Give it some time first. See how you feel." He emerged from the cupboard with a little box in his hand. "What side do you sleep on?"

"I...I..."

"I'd suggest switching for a while. Even to your back. After a couple of days, use the pillow like I said, under your side, OK?"

Lékè stayed sitting and nodded.

In the awkward silence, the physiotherapist shuffled his large feet and cleared his throat.

Lékè stood up and picked up his backpack. "I...I have a sore tooth."

The man frowned.

Lékè continued. "I wonder if you know a good dentist." He smiled and looked to the ground, bashful, as if he'd just asked him out to dinner.

"OK. Sure. Let me... Let's see here." The man walked round his desk and handed Lékè a blue card from the drawer.

"Yes," Lékè said, answering a question that hadn't been asked.

He took the card with an eagerness that made their fingers crash into one another. Amidst his own chorus of apologies, Lékè left the room.

◆◆

"Mister Jack S... Sala..." The dentist stared at the folder in his hand as if it was its fault that he could not pronounce the name.

Lékè had selected the name on the merits of the customer's profile. Now he realized he ought to have chosen a less conspicuous alias.

"Jack is fine," Lékè said and the dentist sighed.

"Hi, Jack. Thank you. I hope you don't take offense, I'm not very good with the African names." His smile seemed fake but his eyes sparkled with warmth.

Lékè shrugged.

"Take the backpack off and sit please. I'll adjust the chair a little."

Lékè sat in the dental chair and leaned back.

"Backpack off, please. Unless you're the one who won the lotto last night? In which case you can hand it to me." He was chatty, a high-pitched squeak of a voice and a distinct Afrikaans drawl to his words.

Lékè removed his backpack.

The dentist tied on his face mask and pulled on a pair of latex gloves. "OK, Meneer Jack," he said, leaning over Lékè. "What's the problem?"

"Somewhere in the back."

"OK. Say ahhh!"

"Ah!"

"Wider please. Is that eina?"

Lékè shook his head.

"Wider. Where do you work?"

"Ah! Oi shee."

"Pardon? Wider."

"Ahh!"

"Perfect. Hold that."

The powdery smell of latex filled Lékè's nose. He linked it with the smooth bitter taste of the fingers in his mouth.

"I don't see anything."

Lékè wondered about the gloves. Why did they need gloves? How could they feel anything with the gloves on?

"Does that hurt?"

He shook his head again. A line of spit seeped out the side of his mouth. The dentist removed his hands and asked Lékè to rinse. He spat. "What are those for?"

"The gloves? Ag, just to protect us."

"From what?"

"Each other, I guess." He laughed. "Open wide, please."

He used a spiked implement and scraped along the sides of Lékè's teeth. Occasionally he used the suction to remove the excess saliva.

"What do you do?" the dentist asked.

"Un-ge-a."

"Pardon?" the dentist said, resting his hands on his knees.

Lékè spat. "I'm an engineer. I work for an oil shipping company."

"Ahh! Interesting, eh? Fun job?"

"Aww." The dentist put his hands down. Lékè spat. "No."

"Ag, shame, man! Ah well—it buys the milk, nê?"

Lékè nodded.

"Open wide again for me, please. Ja, I don't see anything here. Some plaque but that shouldn't cause any pain. You know, sometimes if we miss a floss then bits of food gather and can cause a slight infection. I'll do a basic clean now, OK? And then put the fluoride on." The dentist first scraped then polished.

It felt strange to have someone touch his teeth this way, part his lips, and suck his spit through a pipe. Lékè realized he was bleeding when the dentist asked him to rinse and he spat into the white sink.

"Perfectly normal," the dentist said as he completed flossing in between Lékè's teeth and applied the fluoride paste. "Don't eat for at least half an hour. And I suggest you also make an appointment with our hygienist for about six months' time."

Lékè didn't make a booking for six months. What he desired was a booking for the very next day although he had no reason for the visit. Perhaps he could find another dentist. He could collate all the dental practices in Cape Town and simply go to them one after another. In the middle of imagining this plan, he paused to ask himself whatever was the matter with him. Because—and this he realized as he crossed the street to return for the second half of the work day—there was nothing wrong with his teeth.

◓◒

Lékè rose off the mattress and walked back out to the garden to check on the flowers. Still nothing.

He fell asleep and dreamt of Tsotso staring at him from across a room full of people. When he woke up, it was dark. The flowers, he assumed, had already opened and closed. He'd missed them.

MONDAY 24TH SEPTEMBER 2012

There's a way you simply know. As Lékè's manager approached his desk, he realized he'd been careless. His heartbeat rose.

"Just a quick word, Lékè. A Mr. Jack Salakulandelwa seems to be having some trouble. I see you were the last person in his files. He claims he's been charged incorrectly. The details are all here. Have a look at it."

His manager moved on. Of course he didn't suspect anything, there was nothing to suspect. Yet. Someone (possibly Lewis) had put in another complaint this time about Lékè's tardiness, his unexplained absences. His manager along with an HR assistant had pulled him into a meeting and given him a stern talking to. First that, now this. When he selected Salakulandelwa, Lékè had been certain the customer was what they called dormant, non-active. But apparently Jack was watching his bills very carefully. Lékè was deep in contemplation of how to solve the glitch in his plan when Gene popped up right beside him.

"You scared me."

"Yeah, that's because it's the only way to get your attention. I've been calling you for the past minute."

Lékè pushed aside the papers his manager had left him.

Gene settled his bum on the edge of the table, as if he planned to stay a while. Lékè guessed he was bored which seemed to be Gene's semi-permanent state of being.

"What did Robocop want?" Gene asked.

Lékè shrugged. "Nothing important."

"Speaking of important, did you hear?" Gene asked as he placed his briefcase against the leg of his desk. "They might be changing the interface."

It was the third time Gene was late for work that week. No one ever called him into a meeting about his lateness.

"No, I hadn't heard about that."

There were always rumors of the management changing the operating systems. It was both a security measure and an attempt to keep the company at the cutting edge of the industry. If it were true, it would pose a further challenge for Lékè's plans.

"Well, they are. I'm so pissed off. I just got here, you know? I just learned this freaking system, now I need to learn something else brand new. I mean what the fuck?"

Gene sought Lékè's agreement and Lékè nodded. He wished Gene would return to his own desk. Lékè needed to get into the system and fix his error, find someone really dormant, not this Jack-person. Despite the rain picking at the window, his upper lip began to perspire. Not fully satisfied that Lékè fully appreciated the unfairness of his particular situation, Gene eventually strode back to his desk and swiveled his chair to face his computer screen. Lékè entered the system and selected a Monash Williams. A young girl temping for the week came round placing pamphlets on desks.

"What's this shit?" Gene asked, still sulking, but she ignored him and walked on.

Lékè picked up the one that landed on his desk. It was a flyer promoting some new therapy.

"Hellerwork?" he heard Gene say behind him. "What the fuck is that?"

Lékè scanned the sparse writing. After a few minutes, Gene rose to go to the bathroom. Lékè looked around the office. His neighbor was not at her desk and everyone else seemed preoccupied. He picked up the phone and dialed. When the receptionist answered, he dropped his voice, close to a whisper. "Hello, I'd like to make an appointment...Williams." He rattled off his cell number and waited while the receptionist retrieved the diary. "How about tomorrow?" he asked when she got back on the line. "The next day, then? Oh I see."

The Hellerworker was a renowned practitioner, highly sought after with a three-week waiting list. Depressed, Lékè listened to the receptionist call out the far-off date of his appointment.

He waited out the rest of the working day. At one point, he felt as though his whole body was on fire.

"You sick or something?" Gene asked.

"No, I just–"

"You're sweating and it's freezing outside. Don't get sick on me, man. Here."

Gene tossed a packet of tissues and Lékè wiped his forehead. He was about to try and explain to Gene that maybe he was sick but the moment passed.

"Check it out, Tsotso with the tits is back!" Gene, always going on about women's breasts. Lékè looked to the copy hub, where Gene was pointing. "She was in my orientation session," Gene offered. "She hangs out the back during lunch, chain-smoking. She's hot!"

She was tall but the addition of high-heels gave her a height that couldn't be ignored or forgotten. She seemed oblivious to Lékè and Gene, soaking in all her movements a few meters away with Gene's running commentary for accompaniment.

"Nice legs on her, eh?"

Studying her profile, Lékè guessed that she never smiled. It was a strange thing to notice. He figured he never smiled either but something about her face—it wasn't just that she never smiled, it was as if she couldn't.

"Hey!" Gene shouted across at her.

She looked up from her photocopying and Lékè held his

breath as her eyes passed over them. She jerked her head up in acknowledgment.

"My copier's broken," she said as if they had challenged her presence in their workspace.

"No problem, sweetheart," Gene answered and smiled like Lékè had never seen him do. "When's the next blood thing?" he asked as her cellphone rang.

She kept the phone between her ear and shoulder, talking and copying at the same time.

After she'd left, Gene wheeled his chair closer to Lékè's. "You think she has a boyfriend?"

Lékè shrugged.

"Know where she sits?" he persisted. "I know she's in the legal department. Do you know where that is?"

Lékè pointed down towards the other side of the office. A few steps took you through a passageway and into a separate wing of the building.

"Haven't seen her since the clinic. Clearly she's been busy. Heck, I had that, I'd keep it busy too. Nice," Gene murmured, running the backs of his fingers against his manicured stubble. "Very, very nice."

Gene's leering was obscene. Lékè wanted to punch him.

WEDNESDAY 26TH SEPTEMBER 2012

"What did you think?" Tsotso asked her grandmother, who sat strapped under the seat belt, smiling but not talking.

Tsotso had noticed that her grandmother said less and less these days, but the doctor had warned her about that. "Well, I liked it!" Tsotso answered her own question. "And I don't normally love acapella, hey? Give me string and wind any day. Just the voice on its own—never really interested me. But I guess the voice is an instrument too? Wind, would you say? Makhulu, you listening?"

Her grandmother was fiddling with the seat belt. "I don't like this thing," she said.

"It's a seatbelt. Please leave it, Makhulu. Please." Umakhulu settled down again and Tsotso continued, "I understood something today—good music is good music, doesn't matter what instrument you're using. Could you hear OK? I was worried about you and your hearing aid."

Her grandmother started giggling, at what Tostso could only guess. She touched Umakhulu's shoulder, held her hand there for a few seconds, then focused back on the road.

Just before they turned off the main drag, nearing home, Tsotso broke the silence. "I know Naledi had a voice. I don't know how I know but I just remember red stilettos and Busi Mhlongo on the CD player. But my mother's voice singing louder than Mhlongo's. I didn't know it was Busi Mhlongo until many years later in a bookstore. I asked the guy at the desk and he looked at me like I was crazy. Like no one goes into bookstores and asks about the music they're playing."

Umakhulu bent down to tie and untie her shoelaces. She was humming to herself.

They stopped at a red robot. Tsotso watched her, decided to let her do what she wanted. The light changed and she focused again on the road. "I don't mind really. I don't hate her. It's not so bad to love music more than anything, even your own child. I'm probably the same...except the child part." She hiccupped. One less drink at the bar would have been the responsible thing to do.

Tsotso parked the car and was thankful when Umakhulu, posing no difficulty, let herself be guided through the parking lot.

They stood outside the door to the flat as Tsotso searched for the keys.

"Naledi," Umakhulu said, confusing Tsotso, her grand-daughter, with her child.

"Yes, Makhulu," Tsotso said. She was still searching, too much crap in the bag.

"Naledi," her grandmother repeated and Tsotso looked down at her. The old woman reached up and cupped Tsotso's cheek. "My child," she said.

The words, perhaps the memory of her favorite child, made her face gentle again. Not the harassed look, the tell-tale sign of a tumbling down mind. Tsotso bent down to give her grandmother a hug. This was, after all, a good day.

SATURDAY 29TH SEPTEMBER 2012

The pain persisted. Headache, bodyache, earache. His work kept Lékè distracted but during weekends, with no Plaza Mall, keeping busy was difficult. He decided to take a walk in the streets of his neighborhood.

His favorite street was where Elias's corner shop stood; a narrow road, cobbled, making it unpopular for speeding cars. It seemed more suited to the trendy surrounding suburbs that had been redeveloped but somehow it had landed up amidst the old, creaking neighborhood excluded from the gentrification project. Still, people visited, walking and stopping to drink coffee, browsing the quaint second-hand bookstore, or letting their tongues water over dainty cakes arranged in shop windows. They ignored the beggars and the skollies stretched out on the narrow pavement, nursing hang-overs, careful to sidestep mysterious puddles and avoid eye contact with girls too young to be mothers proffering their crying babies as evidence of their desperation.

The street seemed confused to Lékè, sad to have been left behind. He walked up and down, counting the cobbles. Occasionally he moved to the side for a scooter to pass, or an ambitious loading truck.

He stopped at Elias's store and peeped in, trying to see and avoid being seen. The old man hardly came out in the sun, complaining that his eyes were weak and harsh light could blind him. When he did come out, he wore cracked sunglasses with masking tape holding the frame together. Customers complained of the lack of light in his store; they couldn't see the wares. Elias waved them off, unbothered. People put way too much significance on how things look.

"Feel it, man!" Lékè heard Elias say. Lékè watched him come round from the counter and approach the customer. "Doesn't that feel like quality to you?"

Lékè smiled, pleased that somehow people continued
to come and that Elias's shop stayed open. He stood aside
as the customer walked out through the shop entrance.
She studied what she'd bought and, satisfied, continued
on her way.

"Hey, girlie!" Elias had Whitie on her hind legs.

Standing, the Great Dane matched his height. They
were trying to do the waltz. Whitie barked and Elias cackled—he attempted to hum the tune from Swan Lake but
ended up coughing instead.

Lékè could not look away.

"I can see you, China. You better come in."

Lékè retreated but he heard Elias protest and promise to
hold Whitie down. He walked into the shop.

"How you? Haven't seen you in a while."

"Been busy."

"How's that old crow? She dead yet?" He was talking
about Widow Marais. What was the deal with Elias and
Widow Marais? Lékè had heard a rumor that they'd had
an affair long ago and that the Widow had snubbed Elias
and he'd never forgiven her. "She have a key to your house,
Lékè? Careful that crow doesn't come and kill you in your
sleep. Don't be fooled by the walking stick—strong as an
ox, that one."

Lékè smiled, thinking the rumors must be true. There
was too much feeling in Elias's voice. At the very least, there
was a history—his passion attested to it.

"Come, this nonsense between you and Whitie must
stop! Come, Lékè. Closer, man! Pet her." He took Lékè's
hand and ran it along the dog's coat.

The sleek black hair and twitching muscles, the warmth
coming off her body, surprised Lékè.

"That's a girl. She's a beauty, this one."

"You love her?" He didn't know where the question
came from.

Elias was taken aback.

"Sorry," Lékè said. He'd misspoke.

"No, old man. No, ja, you're right, hey? What can I say,

I love her."

They stood petting the dog together for a few seconds. Whitie had her tongue out and there was only the sound of her enthusiastic panting. Elias had more to say, Lékè could feel it, so he just waited.

"I was there the day she was born. Almost exactly five years ago to the day." He whistled and Whitie barked. "A friend of mine, Marta, breeds up in Malmesbury. Show dogs. Just a few litters a year, not many. They call it whelping, when the bitch gives birth. I'd been bugging Marta for months to help with the births. I've always had an interest; I was almost a vet, you know? You think all I do is sell seed? And I got money stashed away too—I'm not the poor bastard you think I am. Anyway, so Marta finally called up and invited me. Man, Lékè!" He whistled again and Whitie barked. "There's nothing like it. Didn't you see that documentary? Ag, doesn't matter, man. I was there. Now, look at this, see her spots, Lékè?" Elias showed Lékè the marks, pride in his voice. "Aha!" Elias continued, fully into his own tale. "That was funny to me 'cuz I got spots too. Check here." He turned his back to Lékè and lifted the bottom of his jersey. "See?"

Along the left side of his back, just above his glutes, five splodges of taupe-colored flesh. The rest of Elias's skin was a raw pink.

"See, my China?" Elias covered up again and turning back to face Lékè. "Whitie and me, we the same race, man. You get the Blacks, the Whites, the Coloreds, and then there's the Spotteds."

Lékè could still hear Elias's hacking laughter as he walked back up the bridge.

FRIDAY 5TH OCTOBER 2012

Lékè decided on the parking tower opposite the Plaza Mall as his new stomping ground. It was four stories and, on an earlier foray, he'd discovered that from the top floor, he could see the Plaza Mall atrium.

He drove up the sharp ramp deciding, for a change,

to stop on the sparsely lit third parking level. He reverse-parked, turning his head and taking in the view of the Cape Town Harbor with its twinkly lights and its ships. Lékè shut the engine. It wasn't Plaza Mall but it eased his headaches and that was something. He seldom left his car, content to remain concealed and simply study the cars that parked on whatever level he'd chosen for that day, watch the people emerge from their vehicles, watch them walk to the elevator or the stairs. Sometimes there were two in a car or three. Often it was just one person, lugging a laptop bag, groceries. Sometimes they had a suitcase, returning from a long trip, Lékè thought.

He didn't have to worry about over-zealous guards. In fact, it seemed as if there were none. In the short time he'd been coming, he was yet to see a security guard manning the boom or patrolling the grounds.

Sometimes, like tonight, Lékè fell asleep waiting. He woke with a start just past 9 pm. For the next hour, there were no people about and Lékè relished the silence and the darkness. Only an occasional twitch in his face revealed his anticipation.

Lékè leaned forward at the sound of a car revving up the ramp followed by beams of light as it came round the corner. He noted a large man in the driver's seat and another man sitting beside him. They were laughing. They parked on the level above; the car doors slammed and there was continued laughter, fading, as they walked towards the stairwell and then silence.

He waited, his mind light, a weightlessness that moved into his limbs till he felt he might be somewhere in outer space, buoyant and insignificant.

Half an hour later, a woman came from the stairwell and walked towards her car. She was dressed for a party in a short, sequined dress that shimmered. Her thighs were exposed and the rest of her legs, from the knees down, were clad in tight leather boots. Lékè heard the sound of her car alarm deactivate. She drove past, down the ramp to the unattended boom, and was gone. The parking lot was silent again.

Lékè looked at his watch. Almost half past ten. He drifted off and woke again when he heard the bang of a car door. He rubbed his eyes. He could hear mumbling. He wound down the window, cringing as the machinery squeaked. The click clack of high heels and a shuffle. He sat frozen, waiting for something to happen.

"...there you go."

"But what about the rabbits? Shouldn't we wait for them?"

"Don't worry about them, Makhulu. Your bed's made up. Warm bath. Hot tea. What do you say? That's it. Watch your step."

"Hot tea, you say? I like hot tea. But not too hot. Will you blow it for me?"

"Yes, Makhulu. I'll blow it. Let's get inside. It's cold out here."

Their voices carried, bouncing off the concrete surfaces of the dim car park. He looked to the left, from where the voices came. Eventually, they turned the corner and he saw two figures in silhouette, walking down the ramp headed for the double doors of the stairwell. One leaned on the other. They walked through a beam of light and Lékè drew in his breath.

Tsotso looked different, still not smiling but softer somehow. Naked, without a bunch of files in the crook of her arm or a laptop dangling from her shoulder. She had to bend to support the older woman, her arm around her upper back, urging her on. For a long while after the doors closed behind them, Lékè felt he could still hear the uneven tapping of her heels on the ground.

He looked at himself in the rearview mirror as he drove down the ramp. When he smiled, the whiteness of his teeth surprised him.

Driving home, Red's rumble cut through the icy cold. Back in Woodstock, the roads were bare. He'd left the car window down and an icy wind blew in. It was so quiet, he imagined he could hear the houses take a breath between dreams.

Lékè clicked open the garage door and drove Red in.

He hadn't noticed earlier but there was a missed call from Marcus. He'd left a message wanting to know if Lékè was coming on Sunday.

Stepping into his studio, a harsh odor entered his nostrils and Lékè realized his home was filthy. He saw it through her eyes, imagined her walking around inspecting the dark corners, and a sense of embarrassment came over him.

The easy joy of a few minutes ago, the glee, wafted away. Although he sat motionless on his mattress, Lékè's senses were scrambling—hastily trying to sustain the clean scene of happiness. But the stink of his unwashed floors and sticky walls pervaded.

◆◆

Many years after Jane's death, Lékè must have been sixteen or so, he came home from school to find Marcus and a half-empty bottle of whiskey at the kitchen table. It was the only time he ever saw him drunk. Lékè had ignored him, warming his dinner in the microwave and heading for the TV room.

"How come you didn't speak?" Marcus's voice was hoarse and the usual clip in his words wasn't there.

"What do you mean?"

"After she died. How come you did that thing? Not talking." Both hands wrapped around the short glass and Marcus stared into the liquid.

"I don't know."

"Don't you remember? Think back."

Everything had happened so quickly. Maybe words and conversations speed up time, ushering it into always a darker future, crowded with unfamiliar shapes. Maybe he'd used silence as a balm to the uncertainties of life.

"Lékè, I asked you a question."

"I don't know, Marcus. I think I was scared."

"Scared? Scared of what?"

He was young; perhaps he'd thought that if he said

nothing, if he barely even breathed, the world would shrink to a size he could fit into.

"Scared of what, Lékè?"

~ ~

Sitting in his studio, on the edge of his bed, Lékè realized it had worked. The two worlds, waking and sleeping, that it had been his duty to navigate as a boy, had shrunk to the space of a smudge.

His headache returned.

He slept, fell into a charcoal black hole, and emerged exhausted, his muscles aching from a fight he couldn't remember.

SUNDAY 11TH OCTOBER 1992

For Lékè:

I have nightmares about my grandparents' visits to the Babaláwo. Everything happens as if I'm actually there. In one dream, I'm my grandfather and I can feel my wife's clammy palm in mine. In another dream, I'm my grandmother.

There are even times when I'm the Babaláwo; I see everything through his eyes:

"What brings you here?" I say. I can't speak Yoruba so the Babaláwo in my dream can't either. He is yellow like me—ọmọ púpā—with curly hair that springs up after I push it down.

"Ẹ jó 'kó," I say. The little Yoruba I do know is plastered all over my dream—I always have something to prove to my father.

My grandmother places the keg of palm-wine by my feet. The handle is sticky, the red cap is loose, and the cloudy liquid seeps out.

She tells me her troubles. It is not her rash she seeks to cure, or the loss of her hair and her beauty. "Seven boys," she wails.

This is simple, I think. People have come to me before with such requests. They want a boy or they want twins or they want a girl after twin boys. I throw and I start to see the complication in this special case. I throw again. My grandparents crowd me, their sweat drips off their skin and interferes with the Ōdù.

"What is it?" They want an explanation for the frown on my face.

"An old curse," I say. "Forgotten. You will bear only boys."

They shudder because they know forgotten curses are harder to remove than remembered ones. When people curse and forget they cursed, the medicine is left to marinate, seeping into the cursed family—becoming part of their DNA.

Some people would have let this slide, gone home, and lived their lives. Not my grandparents. At any cost, Mama Wōlé begged. She wanted to bear a girl before she died.

"At any cost?" I ask them and human beings are so hungry for whatever it is they are hungry for—both grandparents, Mama Wōlé and Ògá—nodded without a second thought.

THURSDAY 11TH OCTOBER 2012

"I got her number."

Lékè turned his head and then looked back at his computer screen.

"The chick," Gene continued. "Tsotso, I got the digits." He pretended not to hear.

"You listening?"

"How?"

"I have my ways." Gene laced his fingers and stretched his arms out in front of him, grinning.

Lékè continued with his work.

"Don't you want to know if I called her?"

He was trying to keep his breathing steady. "Did you?"

"Not yet. It has to be just right. I'll get her, though, watch me."

Lékè could feel his muscles tightening and he wanted to smack the look of mirth off Gene's face. During his lunch hour, he walked to the back of the Western Medical Fund building. There was a small open car park bordered by grass and some poplar trees bent into submission by the southeaster.

The wind jumbled his thoughts. He liked the feeling. He knew when he returned to his desk, the sense of longing would come back but then it would soon be 5 pm and he could go pick up Red and drive to the parking tower.

A single concrete bench had been constructed on the grass. Lékè sat down and closed his eyes. Even though the wind was cold, a high sun warmed his cheeks and forehead. The smell of smoke alerted him and he opened his eyes.

She was looking straight at him. "You mind?"

He wasn't sure if she meant did he mind her sitting with him or did he mind the smoke. He signaled no. Not seeming to regard his response, she took a deep pull and stubbed out the remaining cigarette with her shoe.

"You drive a red Volvo, right?"

Her voice was husky. It made Lékè think of something that was seldom used. Her skin let off a warm glow, mis-placed with her stern looks—plump but straight lips; flat eyes; hair pulled back off her face in thick cornrows. "I saw you last night and a few other times. I wasn't sure it was you till yesterday."

He'd returned repeatedly since that first night he'd watched Tsotso guide the old woman along. Normally, they got in around 5:30 pm but on a Wednesday and Friday, it was later. He'd wondered where they were coming from so late.

"Are you stalking me or something? Are you some kind of weirdo?"

Lékè could tell no one ever messed with her. In heels, she was taller than him. His eyes looking straight ahead found a spot on her nose. He had to glance upwards to meet her gaze.

"You deaf?"

"No." He flinched, thinking she was going to hit him but she pulled another cigarette from the pack in her shiny leather handbag slung off her shoulder.

She slackened her glare and leaned against the wall.

The garden area marked the end of the office property. It was closed off by a wire mesh fence. Sometimes Lewis could be seen patrolling this border but often the field remained abandoned. Talk of expanding the office—building another wing—and doubling the work force echoed through the tea pause area but nothing ever materialized.

Lékè looked straight ahead. Beyond the fence there was some kind of laboratory and men and women in white coats were constantly crossing the street to buy cigarettes and coffee.

"Why do you go there?"

He'd almost convinced himself she'd left.

"I...I'm sorry. I didn't mean to frighten you." He walked off and avoided her for the rest of the day.

FRIDAY 12TH OCTOBER 2012

"What do you want? What are you doing here?"

Seeing Marcus standing outside his home, Lékè felt descended upon. He'd been working up the strength to call and ask for the brown envelope but this was different. He didn't enjoy being cornered.

"Didn't see you at the grave on Sunday. I ran a bit late, thought maybe I'd missed you or something. Can I come in?" Marcus followed Lékè into the studio.

Lékè had never been in the space with anyone else except Widow Marais's niece when she showed him the place, and even then she'd stood just outside the entrance. It suddenly seemed small with two people inside. He decided to leave the garage door up.

"I brought this for you." Marcus held out the envelope. It was torn in the corners, exposing its contents—crinkled white papers. It was less offensive than the first time Lékè had seen it. The envelope. Marcus had said that Jane wanted him to have it. A peace offering? An apology?

"Where did you get it?"

"It...When we got you, it came along."

An instruction manual for his adoptive parents, but instead of reading it, they'd kept it for him to read.

"What if it was meant for you?"

"The envelope has your name on it, Lékè. That's how we knew what to call you."

Curious, Lékè stepped forward to study the face of the envelope. Marcus angled it. "For Lékè," it said. Then underneath, it said "Lay-kay." It was an instruction manual.

"What kind of name is that anyway?" Lékè mumbled.

It had become a rhetorical question over time. He'd asked it in earnest when he was younger but nothing Marcus said was useful in fending off school bullies. A Google search brought up a motley selection of answers: Lékè was a fashionable clothing brand in Antwerp. There was Albanian Lékè and 1000ALL converted into about 7EUR. It was the name of a restaurant in a Balinese resort. It was a town in Diksmuide— a part of Belgium.

"Take it, Lékè."

The envelope was heavier than he'd imagined and the texture of the brown surface, soft—the dry softness of an old woman's wrinkled cheek.

"What do you say?"

He hadn't been listening even though he'd watched as Marcus made a short tour of the studio and stopped by Red with his hand on the roof.

"Pardon?"

"Let's go for a drive. Come on! When was the last time we drove out together?"

"Maybe another time, Marcus." He wanted Marcus to leave so he could put the envelope down. It felt strange holding it. He wanted to put it down.

Marcus walked back towards the door, then he returned to give Lékè a hug. "See you, son."

Lékè pulled down the garage door, sat on his mattress, and stared at the envelope. He wanted to hide it somewhere but was also afraid to have it out of his sight. Like a naughty child who would get up to mischief once left alone.

Two more hours passed before he tore the flap. Dust came off where the glue had caked like the whisper of a jinni. He pulled out the papers inside and reached for the hanging light switch. They had an uneven texture, thin in parts so the ink seeped through, the scribbled words from either side of the sheets bleeding into each other.

He shuffled through the pages, looking for the beginning, and tried to start reading but his hands wouldn't stop shaking. He put the pages down on the bed but as he studied the words, his eyes clouded. He blinked, thinking he was crying, but nothing came. He looked around the room. He could see Red in sharp focus, the new wipers; he could see the grit on the floor, the screw on the handle of the fridge door, the zip on his backpack. But looking back down at the pages, the words blurred.

He stuffed the pages back into the envelope and got his car keys.

His mouth watered in anticipation as he drove to the car park. Every few minutes, he glanced at the seat beside him where the envelope rode like a dangerous passenger.

WEDNESDAY 14TH OCTOBER 1992

For Lékè:

When I was six, I found a photograph of my parents— black and white which I thought was funny because that is what they were.

How I found it was: after pressing purple and red flowers between the pages of heavy books, I would put them on the shelf and forget about them. And then many weeks later, I'd raid my parents' library. It was like harvesting crops, opening all the books, holding them at their spines and shaking them out. The dried flowers would fall to the floor. And one day, the photograph fell out. It was magic for me. I was certain I had planted a string of daisies in between the pages. When the photo fell out instead, it was as if the book had chewed up my flowers and spat out the picture in their place. I loved that picture. I made my mother read what it said on the back.

I kept the picture, claiming ownership. When I grew older, I decided that it had been taken in South Africa. I made up that it was the last picture my parents had taken of themselves

In South Africa, wildly in love and illegal. They were about to flee and then they asked someone to take a picture of them. Perhaps they thought they would never come back again. They were both smiling. They'd interlaced their fingers and squeezed their joined hands between their cheeks. They pressed into each other and my mother's face would have been flushed pink and my father's smile was beautiful. They did seem happy but there was also something else. Perhaps they pressed too hard against each other. You know, like maybe when you're in bed at night, in the dark with strange shadows in the corners. And you squeeze the blankets extra tight. They were squeezing each other like that.

SUNDAY OCTOBER 25TH 1992

Elaine hesitated at the gate. She tucked her head down and pulled in the smell of the sleeping baby.

The southeaster turned tight corners in the neighborhood of Salt River and rustled the rubbish along the road. A rusting Coke can rolled along with a forgotten plastic bag, doing a strange dance. At the entrance to the building, a rubbish skip overflowed. Occasionally the wind would catch and throw something into the air. Every few seconds, the crash and shuffle of old cartons and bottles on the ground. Above the steel gates hung a wide multi-colored signboard that several summers and repeated rains had bleached. There were cartoon figures and little children. In the center of the sign was written "The Black River Parkway Boys' Orphanage—Sponsored by Coca-Cola."

"Soek jy iets?"

There was an elderly woman standing on the other side of the gate. Elaine never forgot that face, the skin gnarled by time, making her look pointy and crooked.

Elaine shook her head and turned around.

That night, the old woman's worn face floated into her dreams. She'd seen it somewhere before. The realization woke her up—it was her own face, after forty more years of living, tired and dead inside.

She recalled the lines along the cheeks and the wasted bulges beneath the eyes. When she looked in the mirror, she saw this face instead of her own.

SATURDAY 27TH OCTOBER 2012

"E"

"The next."

"F_ P"

"Next."

"T_ O_ Z"

"Next."

"L_ P..."

The voice, in the dark, peeled off the walls of the small room. Each time he said "next," the word slid off the skin of the room and teased from Lékè another slew of letters from the jumbled alphabet.

The hard plastic pushed against Lékè's chin. He tried changing positions but felt locked in by the unwieldy machine. In between instructions, he forgot it was his eyes he was testing, enjoying the sound of the sharp clicks as another lens was moved into place. It sounded clean and made him think of Red's windscreen wipers. Click. Click.

"Perfect," the doctor said with a note of admiration that irritated Lékè.

So there was nothing wrong with his eyes, then.

FRIDAY 16TH OCTOBER 1992

Although Oscar knew his own safety was assured, he dreaded the hour of activity during the day when the prisoners were allowed to roam what was referred to as "the field." It was not a field. It was a patch of dirt, a would-be quad, between the various prison blocks in his wing. That hour was important for the gangs. Apart from mealtimes, it was when they got an opportunity to discuss matters and mete out punishment.

❖

For Lékè:

The exercise yard is brown and the wind sweeps up the dirt. It gets in my eyes and the other prisoners think I'm crying.

"Take a snail of this size." The Ifa priest cupped his hands so his fingertips touched. "Stand under a low shade and pluck it out of its shell. Cover the body in lime and salt, wrap it in these cloths." He indicated strips of dark blue adire, that musty smell reminding me of visits to the tailor and agbadas that never fit.

"Place the ìgbín on a shelf in your store room and don't bother it for seven days. After seven days have passed, every seven hours, squeeze the rag over her tongue." He points at Mama Wōlé but is looking right into Ògá's eyes.

"Seven drops in the middle, here." He touches the center of his tongue. My grandparents watch, mesmerized.

I always wake up sweating, the faint smell of the adire still in my nose.

MONDAY 29TH OCTOBER 2012

3 pm

"Oi! Wake up, dude." Gene snapped his fingers in Lékè's face, startling him into wakefulness. "What, did you go clubbing last night or something? You've been snoring. Drink some coffee, have a smoke, do something. Geeze!"

Lékè shook off his fatigue. Checking his backpack for the envelope, he felt the familiar softened edges and relaxed.

Gene, watching, frowned. "What's up with you and that freaking bag of yours? You're constantly feeling it up. What you got in there? Kryptonite?"

In the bathroom, he put the envelope to rest against his chest, fitting the bottom into the band of his trousers so it was held in place.

5:20 pm

Lékè checked his phone as he drove, straining a little, using the street lights to find the right buttons. Marcus had called earlier and he'd let it go to voicemail.

"How are you? I just wanted to check on you and say hello. See you this Sunday? Bye."

Lékè pressed seven to delete and put his phone back into the cubbyhole. He pulled up the ramp and found his new hiding spot where he hoped Tsotso wouldn't see, crouching behind the large bony steering wheel. The few times he'd returned since she'd confronted him, he'd managed to stay hidden.

MONDAY 29TH OCTOBER 2012

6 pm

Walking her grandmother from the car into the flat was always the most challenging part of the day.

"There you go. One step, two step." Tsotso found that if she counted aloud, it entertained her grandmother, distracted her enough to make her compliant as they walked through the car park. The numbers seemed to enthrall her. "That's it," Tsotso encouraged.

"One, two, three."

"Yes."

"One, two, three." Her grandmother giggled, exposing dark gums and a slack tongue.

They were moving along when Umakhulu tripped on her shoelace which, Tsotso hadn't realized, she'd undone in the car. The old woman's legs crumbled underneath her and Tsotso was pulled down with her onto the hard concrete floor. Umakhulu screamed.

"Makhulu!" Tsotso jumped up and started trying to lift her. She was worried a car would come and run them over but the old woman refused to budge.

She checked for bleeding. There was none. A scratch on the old woman's elbow. Her screams were more calls for attention than indications of pain.

Tsotso grabbed her underneath her arms and tried to hoist her up. "Yoh. You're heavy, Makhulu," she grunted and her grandmother twittered like a bird.

"Can I help?"

She hadn't heard him approaching and her heart jerked. "You frightened me, dammit. Don't do that!"

"Sorry. I thought you might need some help."

She appraised him, moved to one side of her grand-mother, and said, "Take that hand."

Lékè followed her instructions.

"OK, Makhulu, we're getting up now. We're going to feed the rabbits."

◆◆

They heaved the old woman through the parking lot and up the steps into the apartment block. By the time they'd put her to bed, Lékè was sweating. Tsotso offered him some water and he followed her into a kitchen that reminded him of Jane's walk-in clothes cupboard. She opened the fridge door and retrieved a white plastic bottle, indicating with her head that he take a glass from the dish tray.

"One for me too, please. I'm beat." She walked back out to the living room which also served as a dining room. It was a small one-bedroom apartment on the fifth floor of the block. A slice of light from a neon sign came through the window but most of the space was drenched in the shadow of the surrounding buldings. Pushing aside a scattering of sheet music, Lékè sat down on the couch and drew his legs up. He felt a soft bundle of blankets by his ankles and realized he was sitting on Tsotso's bed. A stack of books was piled next to the legs of the couch. He stretched to see the top title. *The Magic of Air: The Principles of Plosive Aerophone Design*.

Something was digging into his bum and when he reached into the cushions, Lékè pulled out what looked like a mini screwdriver.

"Give that to me. I've been looking for that one. 'Scuse the mess."

In the corner of the room, random off-cuts and wood filings surrounded two wooden carcasses.

"I'm moving my workshop down the road, anyway," Tsotso answered to a question Lékè hadn't asked.

He shifted his weight on the thin cushion and the arma-ture dug into his sitting bones. What was he doing there? He couldn't believe she had invited him into her house.

Tsotso switched on the television and put the sound on

silent. Something about the mechanical way she picked up and dropped the remote control made Lékè think she did it all the time, like a ritual.

"I like to have something with me in the room sometimes, you know? TV usually works but often I can't stand what it actually has to say. This is a compromise."

She was soft here, in the house.

"So. You'll have to excuse me. I don't ever have visitors." She swung the glass in her hand towards the bedroom door as further explanation.

"Is that your grandmother?"

She nodded. "She raised me, I never knew my parents." She said it so simply and her tone remained even. Lékè realized he'd never actually said those words to anyone. It had always been a detail that felt like a blight on his life, an embarrassing disfigurement.

He wanted to ask her where they went on Wednesdays and Fridays but that would be admitting his guilt. She'd want to know how he knew and it would be downhill from there.

"And you?" She raised her left eyebrow as she scanned him. "What's your story? Let's start with your name. Lékè. What kind of name is that?"

"It's Lay-kay."

"Oh, I've been pronouncing it wrong. I thought it was like lekker!" She snorted and Lékè smiled.

They each studied the contents of their glasses.

Lékè asked, "Is she sick? Your grandmother?"

"Dementia. Losing her mind day by day. One day she wants to play with the rabbits, the next day she thinks I'm her daughter and she's scolding me for something. Mostly she's with the rabbits though."

Lékè frowned.

"She had a hard life, this one. Her mother left home and never came back. She grew up with her father on a farm in Paarl. She has moments of lucidity when she talks to me about the five rabbits her father bought her on her fifth birthday. Fluffy black things. I think she misses them."

"I'm sorry."

"For what? Don't be stupid. There's nothing to apologize for. So." She put the empty glass down on the coffee table to emphasize the end of one conversation and the start of another. "You know everything about me now and all I know is your name isn't lekker."

Something triggered in Lékè's head and he suddenly realized what the strange smell was. "Are you drunk?"

"We go to the concerts."

Lékè thought she was ignoring his question.

"I take her with me to the concerts. I hate to leave her overnight in Frail Care. I think she likes the music. It calms her."

"You go to concerts?" Is that what they were doing?

"Sure. As many as I can. Don't you?"

Lékè shook his head.

She shrugged. "I get a special deal with the tickets. Cousin of mine works the box office."

Someone in a neighboring flat slammed a door.

"Anyway," Tsotso continued. "Sometimes on the way out we stop at the theatre pub. Milk for her—I know the barman—and a tot for me, you know?" She winked. "Or two. Anyway. No concert today, I stopped over all the same. Just a tot. Or three. They also let me play the piano since I don't have my own...yet."

Lékè sank deeper into the couch. "Sorry."

"Stop saying that. Look, I think the visit's over. Thanks for your help. Stop following me around or I'll call the police, OK?"

They rose from their seats together. Tsotso wavered and Lékè held his hand out to steady her.

"Thanks, thanks. I'm fine. See you at work. Don't fucking tell anybody anything. Bunch of gossips, that place. Fucking bastards!"

SATURDAY 17TH OCTOBER 1992

For Lékè:

I loved the thunderstorms that flashed through the

campus. Sitting in the house, it felt like we were in a capsule. My father explained to me that the thunder is just the sound of stone hitting the ground. Sàngó the God of the sky had thrown it down to earth. Had I done anything to anger Sàngó? my dad would ask and I would shake my head in earnest.

My favorite story was about Èṣù who went to two friends who had just sworn they would never fight or disagree. Èṣù made a man walk between the friends. The man wore an outfit where half was red and half was white. One of the friends said, "Did you see that man who just walked past?"

The other friend asked, "The one wearing the red outfit?"

"No, it was white."

And so the friends fought, they disagreed, each disgusted that the other could lie so. They parted ways.

◆◆

"Lékè, stop it! You'll give him nightmares," my mother would complain but in too-soft a voice to mean business.

My father would wave her off, winking at me.

I did have nightmares. Sàngó and Ọbàtálá would fight. Ōdùdūwà would eat lunch then vomit and out would pour three new Òrìsàs. My dreams mixed up the stories. Ọya would cut off my ear and try and feed it to my mother. Mọ́rẹ̄mí, bitter from losing a son for the prosperity of Ife, would steal me from my mother's arms and take me away to the forest. She wouldn't speak, she'd just hiss and then right before I opened my eyes she'd say: you're mine.

I know that when my father died—his okada hit by a truck—I was nine. I was catapulted into a life that had been waiting for me just beyond the bushes. It grabbed me from the life I loved and thrust on me a new kind of existence. The curse had eaten up my cousins, aunts, and uncles and now it was making a feast of my father.

My mother and I returned to Cape Town. When she fell ill, I wasn't surprised—the darkness was closing in. She was tough, though, and she fought off the disease for a decade before finally surrendering, the sleep of death a relief after the hassle of living.

I was a young man by then, intelligent, with a future but life felt hollow. Only the stories my father had woven around me as a boy colored my dreams. My father and mother became characters in this sleeping world. We played and swam and laughed.

It wasn't comfort because I'd always wake up but it was sweet distraction. It was all I had, no real life, just a dream one.

TUESDAY 30TH OCTOBER 2012

"So, how can I help you, Monash?" Her words formed around the pen she held in the corner of her mouth.

He kept his gaze in front of the homeopath's hands that rested on the desk. He shrugged. When Lékè spoke, she took the pen out of her mouth and scribbled in her notebook.

"I have an eye problem. A reading issue. Sometimes I get a headache from trying to focus. I thought... maybe it's a temperature?"

Jane used to check his temperature. Not with a thermometer but with the backs of her hands. Lékè watched Dr. Meyers write down a few words. He could smell her perfume, rose. Her cheeks were pink and she had on green eye-shadow. Jane would have been about this age had she lived. When the doctor crossed her legs, something jingled—maybe she had bells on her skirt. There was a stack of large grey hardback books to one side of her desk and a terracotta mug filled with unsharpened pencils.

"So you get this headache from reading? Do you read a lot, Monash?"

"No no, it's not from reading anything. It's reading something specific."

"Ah! On your desktop? Have you adjusted it appropriately? Most people use it incorrectly." She raised her grey bushy eyebrows.

"No, it's not the desktop."

"OK. Well, how long have you had this headache?"

"I've always had it but it's suddenly gotten worse."

"Is it continuous?"

"Comes and goes. When I'm reading, I said."

"Ah! All right, I want to ask you a few more questions."

"What kind of questions?"

"Questions about you and your history. Are you familiar with homeopathy?"

Lékè shook his head.

"At the end of our consultation, I'll prepare a remedy for you. But I'll treat the whole of you—not just your headache. Oftentimes conventional medicine treats the symptoms but doesn't consider the cause. I'm not only going to treat the symptom, your headache, but I want to know about you. How you think, how you live. All of those factors could influence what kind of treatment would make a difference. Make sense?" She peered at him with dark eyes.

Sixty, Lékè thought, guessing her age. She wore a blue beret, crooked to the side of her head. Strands of grey kept falling out and she tucked them back in.

After each question, she put her palms together and rested her cheek against her hands, cocking her head sideways as she listened to his responses. She then wrote in her book in some kind of shorthand and asked the next question.

"What are you most afraid of?"

"Like how?"

"Another way of looking at that is what do you avoid?"

"People."

"What do you mean? All people? Just some people?"

Tsotso's face sparked in his mind. "I don't know."

"Are you scared of people, or of what the people could do?"

Lékè shrugged.

Dr. Meyers cleared her throat and changed to a different line of questioning. "What do you strive for, Monash? In life?"

Lékè shrugged.

"What I mean is, what are you always working towards?

What do you struggle with?"

"I...I don't know." This was going nowhere.

"It's possible the reason you can't read is that, instinctively, you don't want to. Some kind of self-defense mechanism. Your body's primordial reaction to a perceived threat. What's the nature of the material you're struggling with?"

"Nothing significant."

Dr. Meyers didn't check his temperature or measure his pulse. She scribbled on her pink notepad and consulted a black volume on the shelf behind her desk. At the end of the appointment, she gave Lékè a bottle of white pills and a stack of powders, folded into twenty pieces of paper, bound together with a rubber band.

Lékè felt that the appointment had been a waste of time. The questions had irritated him—he'd lied in answering most of them. What business was it really of hers? He was scared of people. Not in the usual way. He was scared of what happened between people. Better not to get involved.

Lékè stayed sitting in Red outside the garage door. A familiar car pulled up in front of the Widow Marais's gate and the old woman's niece went up the walk.

He thought of Dr. Meyers and her stupid questions. When he was ten, he'd thought that he ought to have been able to keep Jane alive. It seemed a plausible task to set himself. Keep your mother alive. In the end, it had been easier to keep Red alive instead. And it had worked. But not really. Red was Red, a machine. And no matter how Lékè had tried it and imagined it, you could love a machine all you wanted but you'd be a crazy person if you expected it to love you back.

SATURDAY 6TH OCTOBER 2002

"Get me some water, please, darling," Jane said, pushing Lékè out of the bed.

He returned with the glass. Jane was staring, unmoving, at the ceiling. Lékè laid his hand on her cheek and her eye twitched and startled him. He put his ear to her mouth and a hush came out, small breaths. Strained.

"Mummy?"

"Help me." She raised herself in the bed and Lékè tilted the glass to her lifeless lips.

Most of the liquid poured down her neck. Lékè sat next to her on the bed. "Should I call Dr. Mdu?"

Several months before, Marcus had taken Lékè aside and explained to him, for the first time, that Jane was dying. He'd shown him where he kept the number of the oncologist and said to call if ever anything happened while he was away.

"No," Jane said, but somehow Lékè knew he should. He stayed sitting.

"Should I call the doctor?" he asked after several moments passed.

"It's OK, Lékè. I'm just tired. I need to sleep. Come." They lay down together, Lékè making sure he lay on the wet part of the bed. They stayed silent for what felt like hours. Lékè could tell she was collecting her strength for something. He moved his ear closer to her mouth so she wouldn't have to strain her voice.

"Take care of Marcus, OK?" She was still for a while. "Dear God," she said.

◆◆

Marcus had headed home from George the second he received the call from Lightness, who had discovered Lékè coiled around the stiff body. Arrangements were made and not many words passed between father and son.

"He needs you," Jane had said of Marcus. But, to Lékè, that seemed untrue. In fact, Jane was wrong. He was not needed.

After the funeral, Marcus had left to go off to another conference. He hadn't said goodbye. Ten-year-old Lékè grew up overnight. He resolved to retreat into his own world. He knew he couldn't stay there forever but he'd stay for as long as possible.

Lékè picked up his phone, pushed the button for phonebook, and scrolled down to "Marcus." Leaving the screen on, he laid the phone down beside his bed and went to sleep.

He dreamt that he was a bird flying through a forest. He was flying at a great speed and enjoying the wind as it smoothed down his feathers and the tips of the leaves as they brushed against his breast.

Suddenly a voice sounded out, "Why have you come here? The last time you came, I asked you never to return."

It was a high-pitched voice and Lékè immediately knew he was being addressed by an evil witch. He slowed his flight but stayed buoyant.

"Answer me!" she screeched. "I promised you death on your return and I will not go against my word."

"Do what you must, my Queen. I had to come back."

"Had to? Stupid feathered creature, what do you mean 'had to'?"

"You see, when you banished me, I too gave my word never to come back. But, I love the forest. I love the speed I can achieve here with the wind and I love the laughter I feel when the trees tickle my belly. I am happy only here, so I came back."

SATURDAY 3RD NOVEMBER 2012

Lékè retrieved the broom from beside the fridge and started sweeping. The dust puffed up angrily at the disturbance. After cleaning the floor, he used an old rag to wipe the windows, but the water he'd dipped it in was insufficient. He merely succeeded in spreading the greasy dirt along the pane. He needed to go shopping.

Lékè found himself at the end of the aisle with his basket still empty. He'd already visited Woolworths and doubled his wardrobe by buying four items of clothing. He'd enjoyed squeezing into the small change rooms and studying himself, twitching at the unfamiliar feel of the fabrics on his body. He even bought a belt, drawing the line at the pink-speckled tie the salesman dangled in front of him. Now at the supermarket, there seemed an endless series of options for cleaning dirt. He needed something heavy duty, he thought, leaning in to study the fine writing on the multi-colored labels. His phone buzzed in his pocket.

"Hello?"

"Is this Mr. Williams?"

"Pardon?"

"I'm calling from Dr. Kleinsmith's rooms, the heller-worker. Are you on your way, sir? We were expecting you fifteen minutes ago."

Fuck, he'd forgotten, the freaking Hellerworker.

"Hello?"

"Yes. Yes. I'm sorry. I have to cancel, something's come up."

"We will need to invoice you, Mr. Williams." Her voice tightened.

"Yes. OK. I apologize."

"Do you want to re-schedule now?"

"No. I'll call again. Thanks."

He picked a pink tub with capital red letters along its side—CHEMCLEAN—and two scrubbing brushes with steel bristles. Amonia. On the way towards the checkout, he wandered through the toiletries aisle, picked up a lace bag of potpourri, lavender, and sage.

Although night approached, a warm breeze accompanied Lékè on his walk home. He enjoyed the rare, pleasant weather. Spring had been slow in baring herself. Most of the days came chilled, a sluggard sun making grey mornings and faded out colors on petal flowers. It was an unusual feeling but he longed for the warmth of summer. When Lékè rented the studio, Widow Marais had explained that she'd covered the garage asphalt in a fashionable screed. Over time, this had cracked in places, leaving lines scarring the surface, some wispy spider webs, others wide enough to lose a twenty-cent coin in.

Wondering how to fix the cracks, Lékè went onto his knees and started scrubbing the floor. A dank smell filled the room, rotting flesh—something had died. He prepared himself to find it while cleaning.

Every few minutes, he went to stand by the back door

which he'd left open for fresh air.

Should have bought yellow gloves, he cursed himself, studying the wet dirt that had gathered under his nails.

He scrubbed the windowpane noticing, with a sense of accomplishment, that the clean glass sparkled from the shine of the streetlights outside.

He used a stick to beat the mattress and began coughing as the dust rose off the worn fabric. He turned the mattress on its side and dragged it to the garden, continually hitting it until less and less dust came off.

The underside of the mattress had been chewed away by moths and he made a mental note to save money for a new bed.

At 1 am, Lékè dropped onto the mattress. He fell into a dream where it was very quiet and everything was misty— he couldn't see his hands in front of him, and walked in a stilted march. Amidst the quiet, his footsteps sounded out like thunder, heavy and so booming, it frightened him.

MONDAY 5TH NOVEMBER 2012

"Hello?"

"Dad."

"Hello, Lékè, how are you, son?"

Lékè hesitated, nervous. "Can I borrow some money?"

Lékè was surprised at Marcus's enthusiasm, his readiness as if this was all he'd been waiting for. I'll pay him back, Lékè told himself as he later made transactions to correct things, using as much computer knowledge as he could to hide his tracks. But the truth is, he was no criminal master mind and Lékè know if they looked hard enough, he would be found out. So when his boss approached him that week and took him aside to discuss yet another irregularity, Lékè's heart climbed up into his mouth.

"What do you say?" His boss really did look like Robocop, like his heart was made of metal.

Lékè wasn't sure. If they conducted a thorough investigation, they would find him, fire him, or...worse.

"Hey! I'm talking to you."

"I...I made a mistake. Sir."

"A mistake?"

Really, conducting an investigation was a hassle no one wanted to get into. Robocop was known for being stern but he was also infamous for laziness. The only un-Robocop part of him, his round belly, attested to that.

"With our customers? You think we can afford such foolishness?" He spoke as if he didn't so much run a company as a boot camp.

Lékè stayed silent. Robocop sized him up and dismissed him. Despite real fear in his body, Lékè had to resist the urge to salute.

◦◦

"So I hear you got pulled in. What did Robocop have to say? Hellooo! You there?"

"Questioning."

"What did you do?"

"Shhh!" Someone in a nearby cubicle leaned over the partition.

Gene, still sitting on his chair, used his legs to slide himself closer to Lékè. He dropped his voice to a whisper. "What did you do?"

Lékè shrugged. "Standard procedure, I guess."

Unsatisfied, Gene returned to his desk. Lékè burrowed into his work. If he were found guilty, would they arrest him?

"Oi! Cut it out," Gene said, pointing to Lékè's foot tapping the carpet.

◦◦

At midday, Lékè went to the bathroom, passed the sinks and urinals, and headed for the single cubicle towards the back. He closed and latched the door behind him, took the envelope out, and put it down, careful to avoid a splash of something on the sticky tiles.

The seat was poorly fitted and the cover fell onto his back when he sat down. He dug his elbow behind him to keep it upright.

Tsotso was with him, the way she always was. He could feel the weight of her on his lap, her backside pressing against his thighs, his trouser zip. With his free hand, Lékè stroked her head, the ridges of the braids like Braille, her neck bent backwards. He could smell her. He could—

"Lékè, you in there?"

What did Gene want?

"Lékè? I'm popping out for lunch, you want something? I'm going to the Indian place."

Tsotso dissolved, and the acerbic smell of mothballs returned.

At the end of the day, Lékè's manager called him in again. "I've decided that there won't be an investigation this time…but I'm watching you. One wrong move…"

Robocop did not need to finish his sentence.

TUESDAY 3RD NOVEMBER 1992

"Hello? Hello?" Jane checked to see if the line had been dropped. "Hello?" she said again and heard someone clear their throat. "Hello, who's that? How did you get my number?"

"It's Elaine."

"Who? Elaine who?"

"Elaine. From the post office. The hospital. Remember? The little boy. You're my sister."

"Oh my God, Elaine! Gosh! How are you? Goodness, your boy must be big now? Five months?"

"Almost three months."

"Lovely. So good to hear you. What a surprise!" The events of that day had stayed with Jane. She thought of it fondly. Only sometimes late in the night, she wished it were her on the delivery bed. In those moments, she suffered the memory, crying into the pillow so as not to wake Marcus.

"Yes, Jane. I thought of you."

"Thank you. How is the baby?"

"He's good. He's big, really big. Growing."

"What's his name?"

"Lékè."

"Oh, that's an interesting name. How lovely."

"From his father."

"How is your husband?"

After a few seconds, Jane heard crying and remembered that the baby's father was in prison.

"Oh, I'm stupid. Sorry, Elaine. I'm sorry."

"Can I come to see you? Can I meet you somewhere?"

Would she bring the baby, Jane wondered? Since her last miscarriage six months before, Jane had experienced the need to both be around babies and avoid them. Driving past a crèche, she had burst into tears. When she'd elected to drive Elaine to the hospital, she'd been a bit worried but her emotions had remained steady that day. For several days afterwards, though, she'd woken up with nausea, and noticed a slight swelling in her belly. Her nipples grew tender. In the morning after Marcus had risen for the shower, she held herself, cradled the emptiness in her arms.

"Please? Let's meet."

"Yes. Let's do that, why not. When and where?"

"Tomorrow? Can I meet you at Hendelsen, off Viljoen Street in Goodwood?"

"Oh goodness, where's that?"

"There's a Stodels on the corner and a park opposite. It's a quiet road. We can meet at the coffee shop next to the park."

"Hendelsen. Hendelsen Road? Let me write that down."

"Thank you. 7 am? I need to see you before work. I hope that's not too early."

"Oh boy! Let's make it 7:30 am. I can sit and wait for the Stodels to open. I need some soil anyway."

"Thanks."

"OK. Take care till then."

A sense of unease followed Jane after she put the phone down but she couldn't decipher it. Her sleep, as usual, was shallow and when her alarm went off at 5:30 am, Marcus complained, "What's going on?"

"I'm going into town early today. Need to run some errands."

"At half past five in the morning, Jane? What's going on with you, you've been shuffling in bed all night?"

"Sorry. It's nothing, Marcus. Go back to bed. I'll give you a call later."

◆◆

The N1 traffic slid along with an ease that would slow to a crawl in another hour. Jane felt relieved that the appointment was early and a tension released somewhere in her body. She turned on the radio, switching from the news to a music channel. Hendelsen Road looked frozen in time, misplaced as though the quaint baskets of bright plastic flowers drooping from the balconies above the strip of shops belonged somewhere in Newlands and not in Goodwood. A grey haze hung low over the narrow street. She drove past the Stodels at the corner. A woman in a white bonnet was sweeping the pavement in front of a café. Jane noticed a figure sitting on a bench in the park, a woman straining her neck, watching the road, and when Jane stuck her head out of the car window, Elaine recognized her and waved.

"Let me park. I'll join you," Jane shouted as she pulled off the road.

She grabbed her bag and turned her car alarm on. As she walked towards the park, she dug her hands in her pockets. A bite still heralded the mornings despite summer around the corner. She stepped over the low bar cordoning off the park area.

"Elaine?" The bench was suddenly empty.

Jane walked towards the bench she'd just seen Elaine wave from.

"Elaine?" she said again and gave a quick look around the small park but it was empty.

Back at the bench, she noticed a large bundle. She immediately knew what it was. She looked around, still expecting Elaine to come running with some excuse about having to dash to the bathroom.

The baby moved and the cloth bundle came awake with gurgling sounds. Jane opened a small gap in the blankets and saw that Elaine had been right—he had grown.

"Lékè," Jane said, smiling and crying.

And she hoped something she knew she would never admit to anyone, not even Marcus. She hoped Elaine was gone and was never coming back. Even if it meant she were dead. She hoped this was final and she made a small pact with a God she seldom spoke to, that if it were final, and if this day could go unnoticed, she would bring up a kind and good person. Someone with a generous heart to make up for her own greedy longings. She collected the baby boy from his packaging and held him to her chest.

FRIDAY 16TH NOVEMBER 2012

1:15 pm

Lékè offered Gene the regular rusk at lunchtime.

"No," he said, leaving Lékè standing with the biscuit.

A few minutes later, Lékè got up to make himself some tea. Gene's coffee mug was empty.

"Leave it," Gene snapped when Lékè picked up the mug.

"Are you OK?"

"Someone said they saw you chatting to your new friend."

Lékè stared at Gene, confused.

"You knew I liked her. I wouldn't have pegged you, Lékè, for the kind to go behind a person's back —"

"Hey! There's nothing going on. I swear."

Gene was wrong, Tsotso mostly ignored him. Since his visit to her apartment, she'd approached him a few times during lunch but he'd failed to carry through a conversation with her. In the past few days, she appeared to have stopped noticing him altogether.

"Ag! It doesn't matter," Gene said, turning back to his work. "Do what you want. Plenty of shrimp in the ocean. And plankton and...argh, fuck it, man, whatever!"

Lékè shook his head and wandered off to the kitchen. He made his tea and left it standing while he went to the bathroom. The envelope chaffed his skin when he walked. He worried that his sweat would ruin the paper. So what if he couldn't see the words, he still wanted the writing intact.

Despite his earnest protestations, Gene spoke little to him for the remainder of the day. Lékè wished Gene's jealousy was called for, but the reality of his lack of relations with Tsotso pressed heavily on him.

◄►

5:30 pm

The directions to the hellerwork practitioner had been easy. Lékè sat waiting on the couch. He looked down a short corridor which ended in a glass door with a fan light. Outside was a garden and Lékè could make out the sunflowers in the fading light. The receptionist was on the phone. When he'd pushed the door open, she'd signaled for him to sit down.

His cellphone vibrated. It was Marcus. He let it go to voicemail.

The receptionist put her hand over the receiver and said, "Lékè? She's running a little late. I'm sorry, sir."

He nodded and she returned to her conversation, tugging at the scarf on her head. When she put the phone down, she apologized again. "Would you fill this out please, sir?"

On the line where they asked how he would be paying, he ticked, "Cash."

A few minutes later, a tall woman with orange-brown dreadlocks came out of the back room. A shorter woman came out with her and went to settle her account. "I'm Ruth Kleinsmith," the taller woman said as she approached Lékè, and they shook hands. "Would you come with me, please?"

The small room had a door to one side and in the middle was a low bed with a white towel spread over it.

"Just put your backpack down there. Then follow me. Before we start, I want to see you walk."

Lékè stared at her, confused.

"Do you know what hellerwork is?"

He shook his head. He couldn't remember the blurb on the flyer, something about posture. What had attracted him to this place had been their willingness to do consultations after working hours. He didn't care about hellerwork. He hadn't slept through the night since Marcus had delivered the envelope. The writing scrawled on the thin paper remained undecipherable—fuzzy. His body ached and he longed for the touch of Tsotso's skin on his. Whatever he'd read on the flyer must have sounded like it would bring some form of relief. Although, now he wasn't sure anymore.

"Is that clearer now?" Lékè heard her ask.

He'd missed her explanation but he feigned a smile and Ruth smiled back.

"OK, Lékè. Come with me. Let's see how you walk."

Lékè followed her through the door. She instructed him to take his shoes off and asked him to walk along the narrow passageway towards a mirror at the end of it. He obeyed, already upset that the appointment would be a waste.

"How does that feel?" she asked. "How do your arms feel? And your waist? Try swinging your hips like this." She demonstrated for a few seconds and then let Lékè try again. "Where's your weight now? Where do you feel it?" she asked.

Lékè answered as best he could, struggling to concentrate. Eventually they returned to the small room.

"Please, take off your shirt and trousers. Leave on your underwear."

Lékè hesitated. The last person who had seen him naked was Jane and that was fifteen years ago.

"I'll leave the room for a short while." Her tone a combination of professionalism and gentle compassion.

On her way out, she said, "Here's a gown you can wrap yourself in. I'll only expose the part of the body I'm working on at any particular time."

The door snapped shut behind her and Lékè stood alone in the room. He looked around. In all the doctors' rooms he'd been to, he'd noticed the posters they taped onto their walls. A picture of infected gums, bleeding. The Desiderata: "Go placidly..." and "Strive to be happy."

On the walls of the hellerworker's room was a picture of the skeletal system and another of all the muscles in the body—a woman with no skin, and arrows, and lettering.

Lékè studied it, snatches of her explanation coming back to him. She worked with the deep connective tissue of the body, releasing "history," she called it. He leaned forward. There was a proverb printed in big capital letters stuck on the wall: There is no cure that does not cost (Kenya).

Ruth knocked on the door and Lékè jerked in fright. "You done, Lékè? Can I come in?"

"No," Lékè said. He unzipped his grey trousers and un-buttoned his long-sleeve shirt.

When Ruth entered the room, she asked him to lie on the bed on his stomach. She wrapped towels around his body, leaving his left arm exposed. She took a small trans-parent bottle and deposited two drops into the palm of her hand and then rubbed her hands together. A sweet smell filled the room.

"It's arnica," she said.

She began to work her hands along his exposed arm. She massaged the palms of his hands and his shoulders. She continued to work in this way, revealing different parts of his upper body and kneading his flesh. She worked with the sides of her hands and the base of her thumbs and her fingertips. She stopped only in moments to rub more arnica oil on her hands.

"How's that? How does that feel?"

Lékè didn't respond. He liked the feel of her fingers spreading the oil on his skin. It felt close and real, not a dream, not a fantasy.

"I do need you to talk to me a little bit," Ruth said. "What are you feeling?"

"Uhm...I'm not seeing so well," Lékè blurted out which was not an answer.

"Okay. You mean—"

"I don't see the letters. I can't read them."

Ruth didn't answer and despite enjoying her touch, Lékè felt sad; he had polluted the appointment with his confusion.

Only when he was paying at the reception did Ruth put a hand on his shoulder. "We can't always see everything,

Lékè." And it felt like a blessing. Lékè left the hellerworker
with those words sharp in his ears—her words permitted a
mystery to life, said he didn't need all the answers. Tucked
so in the layers of his confusion, he could never have imagined such a grace.

∞

11:30 pm

Lékè stood waiting outside the apartment door. Was
it the correct number? He hadn't thought to memorize it
the first time. He'd rung the bell twice already. He pressed
again on the black button and was stepping back when
the door opened. She wore a pink robe over a chocolate
brown slip that had a sheen to it and she was barefoot.
The floor must have been cold. She curled her toes up and
clasped her arms over her chest, rubbing and squeezing
her shoulders.

"What the hell do you want? It's the middle of the night,
Lékè, for God's sake."

It had seemed so sensible when he'd thought of it but
now, standing in front of her, words left him.

She rolled her eyes and opened the door. "Well, come
in while you're thinking of an answer, it's cold out there."
The apartment was as clean as before but Lékè felt less
embarrassed thinking of the bag of potpourri resting on his
window ledge at home.

"So, what do you want? Quickly!"

"I need your help." Humor drained from her face and
for a second, Lékè realized how she saw him. "I know this
is strange. I'm sorry to come like this. I need your help with
something."

"At this time of night? This couldn't wait till working
hours? What's that?"

Lékè brought out the envelope. "Can I leave this here?"

"What?"

"Can I...I'll put this down here."

"What are you talking about? What is it?"

"Letters."

"I don't understand you."

"I can't sleep. But I can't throw them away. I need one night's rest. I'll come back and get them in the morning."

"You're crazy."

"No, no. It's not that. I...they haunt me. I can't sleep, and when I sleep, I have nightmares. If I leave them here, I'll sleep better. I trust you to look after it. I can't trust anyone else." He held the envelope out to her.

Tsotso stood still for a few seconds then moved forward to accept the offering. She examined the contents of the envelope. "What's in here? Letters?"

Lékè nodded.

"Haunts, you say?"

"Please. Just tonight. Tomorrow's Saturday, I'll come by first thing."

◐◑

For the first time since she'd met him, Tsotso studied Lékè's face. His eyes were light brown and soft, nothing about him said outright lunatic, but she'd read the news. It was always the "nice quiet guy" or the neighbors saying, "We could never have guessed." She remembered some advice her grandmother had given her in more lucid times. She checked for any signs of neglect in his bushy afro, nothing. Dirt under his fingernails though. She remained cautious.

"Letters from whom?" she asked.

"I don't know. My first parents." He thought of himself as a second-hand car.

"You're adopted?"

Lékè nodded.

Tsotso considered this.

"You ever met them?"

"No."

"And now they've sent you this?"

"Something like that."

Tsotso gave a loud sigh, utterly confused but too tired to argue any further. "Just for tonight then?"

"Thank you."

◐◑

He didn't dream. One moment, he was studying the shape of the fridge in the dim light from the street and then it was 11 am.

Lékè waited for Tsotso in the parking lot, as they'd agreed.

"Morning." She handed him the envelope.

Lékè opened it and pulled out the stash of papers. He glared at the pages, disappointed to find that the letters were still blurry.

"Everything OK? Listen, I got to collect my grandma from the clinic; I can't do crazy this morning." She opened the back seat of her car and placed her bag on the floor.

"Will you read them to me?" Lékè asked, coming behind her as she prepared to get into the driver's seat.

THURSDAY 5TH NOVEMBER 1992

Elaine had been watching Jane for a few days before she phoned her. She'd looked for her home address in the phone book and been bold enough to take a taxi to the neighborhood. She needed to check her out although she didn't know really what she was hoping to decipher by simply watching a woman enter and leave her home in her Red Volvo. Of course she was looking for kindness. Without a car of her own—and even at that, without a license—it was impossible for Elaine to stalk Jane the way she really wished to. But she did work out that the woman taught science in a nearby boy's school. Elaine watched in the park from across the street. Again she didn't understand what she hoped to learn by watching a woman walk across a field. Her heart pained her. The task ahead was important. Grief was climbing through her like a rash. When she held Lékè to her face, she whispered to him, let him know it was her intention to come back for him, to return.

WEDNESDAY 22ND OCTOBER 1992

For Lékè:
Where did I leave off?
Soon after my grandmother visited the Babaláwo and

followed his instructions, her belly grew and, on the day
when the doctor said to her, "Ōbìnrīn," she wept and wept
for days. My father joked that his sister was fed milk and
tears for the first week of her life.

Āyò was her name but the joy did not last. When she
was three, the Babaláwo came to Mama Wōlé and Ògá's
house.

In this dream, I am my grandmother. I greet him. There
is nothing to be afraid of until he explains his visit and then
there is much.

"You said at any cost," he reminded me.

He wanted Āyò—that was the cost. I could have her for
three years and he would have her for the rest, rear her as his
own child with dignity, and train her in his medicinal ways.

I refused. The Babaláwo did not insist and he did not
force me to give up the baby, instead he bowed and walked
away.

Three days later, Āyò died in my arms. I ran to the
Babaláwo's compound but he was gone. That was the beginning of the darkness.

One by one my sons died, the sons their wives had
borne and their wives too. No more girls were born into the
family and I knew that no more would ever be born.

A few years would pass between each death but it never
abated. One quiet day, after burying four children, I took
my own life and my husband followed me.

I hate this nightmare. This one I wake up panting as if I
have been running.

My feet ache.

THURSDAY 23RD OCTOBER 1992

So that was the darkness. My grandparents made a
deal with the Babaláwo (at any cost) and then they broke
it. When you break a deal, especially with a Babaláwo, you
pay. That was the darkness. This is it here, now. And wherever you are, Lékè, when you read this—that's it there too.

After my mother died, I saved enough money and returned to Nigeria. I was a Nigerian, after all. I went home

and stayed. It was a lonely place, Lékè. I was following my father's instructions—the only way he could think of to keep me alive—which was to live alone and starve the curse of the lives it needed to feed on in order to thrive. My father was very clear, I was not to invite love because even the smallest spark would incite the curse into another spate of deaths.

◄►

And yet there I was when I met your mother—a man at the mercy of love. I permitted it, I went against my father's warnings. And then suddenly there you were; we were bringing a child—I knew you would be a boy—into the world. Another life to suffer? I was prepared to do anything so that we could be a normal family. I needed to go to the monster and look him in the eye—vanquish him. I thought I could reverse the curse. I don't think it worked though. If you are reading this then, wherever you are, I'm not there, so it hasn't worked. I had to try though, Lékè. I'm sorry, son, but I had to try.

SATURDAY 17TH NOVEMBER 2012

"Sjoe!" Tsotso covered her yawn with her forearm. "I'm tired."

"Thank you for this."

"Ag, doesn't matter. I had nothing to do anyway and it's...kinda odd but cool."

"Where's your grandmother?"

"She wasn't eating. I couldn't get her to eat, I've always been able to get her to eat. It got worse so they suggested I leave her in Frail Care for a few days. 'Observation,' they call it."

"I'm sorry."

Tsotso nodded, wiping her eyes.

"I'm sorry," he repeated, suddenly noticing her tears and shifting his weight on the seat.

"I miss her."

Lékè continued shifting in the seat, crossing his legs at the knees and uncrossing them. Tsotso, sitting opposite on the carpeted floor, put her head back against the couch behind her.

"She raised me. She looks small now, hey, but she was athletic. She used to play table tennis, my grandmother." Tsotso cackled and slapped the side of her thigh, pulled up to her chest. "That one!"

Lékè thought not to make a sound. He was afraid that if he did, Tsotso would remember he was there and stop talking.

"Her father had taught her to play and she taught me. We'd play on the kitchen table after dinner with pieces of wood cut from chairs and things. It was fun." She shook her head slowly. "Fuck."

"I'm sorry."

"Stop saying that." Tsotso turned to face Lékè. "You're a fucking stuck record. 'I'm sorry, I'm sorry.' What's wrong with you? Can't you say anything else?"

Pinned to his seat by her angry glare, Lékè felt that his skin might start to fry. She released her gaze, turned back to face the silent TV and the window behind it with Cape Town spread below in a spray of lights. She sucked her teeth, alerting Lékè to the fact that she wasn't done yet.

"What? What is it? What's wrong with you that makes you so sorry? You're sorry. You're sorry?" A new wave of anger propelled her to her feet. She walked to the window then turned again to look at Lékè. "I hate that. Take your stinking pity and suck on it. I don't need your sorry. I thought I could just talk to you. I was just talking."

"I'm—"

She took a step closer and Lékè's words tapered. She felt the cool from an open window blow on her neck and her heart settle. Maybe she'd overreacted. She moved back to the couch and sat down in the same position, not looking at Lékè. The silence was the discomfort of having expressed the intimacy of anger too soon. After more minutes passed, Tsotso gave up wondering what to say. "I'm tired. Are you going home?"

"No."

"Well, I'm in the bed. There's a duvet over there for you on the couch."

Lékè stood in the darkness of Tsotso's living room. A light came under the door from the public passageway, and another blue light from a nearby nightclub poured through the window, along with the repetitive thud of house music. The door to Tsotso's room was ajar. He pushed it open. She lay face up, her left hand hanging off the side of the bed. He watched her chest as it rose and fell, her plump lips parting with the emission of each snore. An occasional bubble formed and popped.

She moved and he stopped breathing for the time it took her to turn her head and resettle her body. Her snoring resumed; his breathing resumed. His eyes moved from her legs to her arms; he could see the soft pulse at her throat. Her feet stuck over the end of the bed, exposed from under the duvet. He wondered whether she felt the cold. When he bent down to pull the blanket over her feet, he noticed she wore a ring the color of copper on her middle toe. Lékè moved closer, hoping the ring would be easy to work off without waking her.

The first time he'd ever taken something came back to him. He'd hidden the photograph of the strange woman. The one he'd found in Jane's cupboard. He kept on telling himself he'd find the right time to ask about it and then he realized that the longer he held on to it, the more impossible it was to give it back.

After Jane died, he decided to never give it back, reasoning, in a way he couldn't explain, that the photograph belonged to him. Like a gift Jane intended to give him but had forgotten to. It was like that when he took things—that's how he thought of it. Taking things.

With nimble fingers, he slowly loosened the toe ring at the gap in the band and then started edging it off her toe. Bit by bit. Eventually he was holding it. The surface of the copper that was exposed to her skin, her sweat, had turned blue in places, a beautiful coloring book blue that reminded Lékè of his childhood. He thought he'd put the ring somewhere safe, in his pocket, then transfer it somewhere even more safe when he got home. But instead he found himself working it back onto her toe. He squeezed gently so that the gap closed. The ring fit snug again.

Lékè studied it on her toe for a few more seconds then tucked Tsotso's feet under the blanket and snuck in beside her.

◆◆

"Did you spend the night here?"

Lékè wanted to look away but her eyes had the power to keep him pierced in place.

Their faces were inches apart and he could feel her breath on his face. Warm and pungent, small specks of muck in the corners of her eyes from the night's sleep.

He wanted to reach and touch her. He was still deciding which hand to use when she sighed, turned, and reached for the stack of letters on the floor by the bed.

"By the way," she started, looking at the pages in front of her, "you can tell the people at work whatever you want. You can tell them that we're friends." She flipped through the remaining pages, as if assessing what they had already read through and checking to see what still lay ahead. "This curse stuff, you think any of it is true?"

Lékè shrugged.

"And what exactly is the curse? What happens to you?"

"Not just to me. But all the people around me."

"What?"

"I can't have a good life. I die, alone and forgotten. And everybody else close to me, they die too."

"Don't you think that's just life, though? Isn't that just how things are? I mean, come on, we all die."

Lékè didn't know.

FRIDAY 29TH NOVEMBER 1991

Elaine ignored Oscar for four weeks after the first time he tried to kiss her. Summer was fully formed and the sunshine set upon the campus, unrelenting and fierce. Evenings were still, and the ground radiated the warmth collected through the day, back into the atmosphere.

8 pm on Friday, Oscar was still marking scripts at his desk, unwilling to go home to his empty house. Elaine knocked on his office door, uncertain he would be in but hopeful.

"Yes."

She opened the door and stuck her head through. A flash of unexpected rain had caught her and she was dripping water onto the carpet.

"Can I come in?" she asked, still standing at the door.

She seemed shy although they'd spent many nights in his office, chatting until late. Oscar nodded a response and Elaine shut the door behind her. She put down the Shoprite bag which held a container of food for her supper. She leaned one hand on a bookshelf while with the other she bent down and removed her shoes. It was getting dark outside and the building was empty.

"You're all wet," Oscar said, noticing the tremble in his own voice.

Elaine shrugged. After she removed her shoes, she sat on the floor, facing Oscar who was still sitting on his chair. He swivelled it out from his desk so that they were facing each other with nothing in between them. She brought her knees up and removed her socks.

"I'm sorry about the other day," Elaine said as she removed her cardigan. "You said you wanted to kiss me. I wasn't trying to...I was just..."

"I didn't mean..." Oscar began.

He stood up and sat down again, unsure where to look. His tongue in his mouth felt like the trunk of the tree outside his office and his limbs were like its roots trapped under volumes of soil.

She removed her vest and stood up so that she could step out of her corduroy trousers. The light in the room flickered. Elaine continued removing her clothes, one layer after the other. Oscar watched, intrigued, wondering what she was doing. When she was almost naked, in her bra and underwear, she walked towards him and took his hand.

"This is all," she said. "I just wanted you to see me. All of me."

She guided his hand along her body. Half of Elaine was beautiful.

"Look at me."

There were two halves of her. Half that was burnt. Half that was not. The burnt skin was calloused and glistened, uneven in parts, as though it had once bubbled and then frozen in place.

"What happened?" Oscar asked. "Somebody did this to you?"

Elaine nodded. "Doesn't matter anymore, I survived. I'm here."

"Does it hurt?"

"Not anymore. Give me your hand."

Oscar relinquished his right hand which she guided along her body, moving from one side to the other, hard thickened burnt flesh to smooth pale freckled skin. Oscar pulled Elaine towards him, into the chair. He whispered into her ear, "You're beautiful. All of you."

They lay down on the long couch in the corner of Oscar's office and fell asleep, covering their bodies with a blanket. A few hours later when they woke up, the sky was purple. Elaine locked the office door. Oscar kissed her neck and her breasts. She sat astride him and they made love.

WEDNESDAY 19TH FEBRUARY 1992

Oscar switched off his engine. His hands shook and he rubbed them together, pretending to himself, despite the still evening, that he was just cold and not scared. He brought both hands to his head and rubbed his palms back and forth over his no. 2 buzz cut. For a few seconds, he enjoyed the spongy sensation of his scalp. He rolled up the windows. The moon was slow in rising and the lights in the suburb were sparse.

Not only didn't Feathers hide his address, he also clearly didn't believe in barricading himself. There were no dogs or guards.

All the houses in the neighborhood either shouted luxury or whispered wealth in hushed tones behind velvety walls, grassy verges hissing and ticking with timed sprinklers. Number thirty-nine sat far back from a medium-high brick wall. There was no one in the streets and cricket noises chirped from the brush as Oscar shut his door and walked towards the house. The gate had no lock. He undid the latch and let himself through. The plan was to knock, look at the monster, vanquish. But, when he reached it, the varnished wooden door was ajar. Oscar pushed it open, no squeak of rusty hinges. Oscar stood in the doorway for a few seconds. He'd never seen a photograph of Malcolm Feathers but had imagined him many times. A big man although he would now be in his mid-eighties, surely no longer a threat. In the absence of a real one Oscar had created his own image of Feathers—a monster from Fágúnwà's *Forest of a Thousand Daemons*. Oscar imagined a sticky deposit on whatever Feathers touched, something oozing out of his pores, the same vapor that wafted off his tongue when he spoke and trailed behind him as he walked.

Beyond the light in the entrance hall, which Oscar had seen from the road, the house was in darkness. As Oscar took one step deeper into the house and then another, he thought of all the things that had happened here. He thought of the burns Feathers had inflicted on Elaine and the less visible scars—her panic if Oscar ever looked too long at her, the paranoid way she covered herself.

In a room off to the side, a chandelier with bulbous crystals hung low. They sparkled but gave off little light. The parquet flooring gleamed, leading further down a passageway. There were steps to the left side of the passageway going down into what looked like a basement. To the right was a staircase leading upwards. Oscar heard something from the floor above and started climbing. What was he doing? His mind was talking but his feet did what they wanted.

On the landing, he turned right and stood, frozen.

It was clear to Oscar that the man standing in front of

him was Malcolm Feathers—an overweight, slow being. He was naked, just coming out of the shower, dripping water from his shaggy head of grey hair and a towel loose around his flabby waist, exposing part of his thigh and a shriveled penis. This was the monster; his joints were swollen, ravaged by arthritis.

Propelled by fright, Feathers moved with a haste his body was unprepared for. He slipped on the expensive smooth porcelain tiles. The sound of his legs sliding and a heavy thud as his skull glanced off the edge of the basin and hit the floor. His body was shaking as Oscar walked into the bathroom. A shiny pool of blood spread onto the yellow floor mat and the wriggling slowed until it felt as though the only sound in the house was a clock ticking. The man's face was not yet drained of all color but his lips were blue. Oscar went onto his knees and put his ear to Feathers's mouth, averting his eyes from the grey saucers, wide open and staring. A warm breath, short.

"Help," Feathers whispered.

Oscar rose up off the floor. He knew instinctively that he would wait, he would wait and watch the breath grow faint, disappear altogether.

"Malcolm?"

Oscar's head jerked as he heard an elderly voice call up towards the landing from downstairs. Should he run?

"Malcolm, we started without you. The boys said you can join the next round. Come on, a shower shouldn't take that long. What are you—"

She was elderly, although she did not look as old as Feathers. She wore red lipstick that was like an x-mark amidst the slack lines of her wrinkled face. Her nails were painted and milky pearls jangled down her front. She was small; he could push past her.

"Who are you? What have you—" Her face contorted as she saw the blood and her friend on the floor, motionless. Oscar's thoughts of running were mired by her screams and the sound of approaching feet.

SATURDAY 24TH OCTOBER 1992

For Lékè:

There is another version of Mọ́rẹ̀mí's story. It is not in the history books—I made it up myself. In my version, the gods longed for love, not grief. Mọ́rẹ̀mí went to the river and cradled her baby one last time before setting him down on the dry banks and jumping into the flowing water.

The gods were appeased. They feasted on the bountiful love she had for her son. And, even today, whenever the waves come onto the banks and lick the sand, that is the gods still feasting.

◅▻

Oscar put the pen down and folded the letter twice. He placed it in the large brown envelope where he'd kept his other letters to Lékè.

As he put the envelope away, he noticed a commotion at the back of the cell. Some of the older gang members had been in prison their whole lives, their families forgotten. The process of visiting, when Oscar enquired, was an arduous task that almost ensured families slipped away and prisoners were left to cleave to one another. The gangs and the violence connected them.

Oscar winced at the sound of a fist hitting flesh. His nerves were fraying and he clasped his hands together to stop them from shaking. Some strange luck had won him immunity but he was doomed to live out his sentence, watching others who were less fortunate being beaten and raped. Each day less of him remained for the people he loved.

Looking around him, as though for the first time seeing his circumstances, Oscar realized this was the darkness. The curse killed off families, connections, and intimacy. Here he was in prison. Yes, he was still alive, but there was no heartbeat to the life he'd been left with, no warmth. He would finally see Elaine in eight months' time, but which Oscar would she come to visit? Which Oscar would this place serve up for her? He got up off the bed. There was nothing left to do. He'd defend the young boy being raped behind the curtain. He'd do what was necessary to become human again.

SUNDAY 25TH OCTOBER 1992

In the week, unexpectedly, Elaine had received a call from the lawyer saying an early visit had been negotiated due to Oscar's good behavior. That had been Wednesday or was it Thursday. Strangely Oscar himself had not been informed yet but the lawyer mentioned that come Monday, Elaine could visit. She'd worked all of Saturday, cleaned three houses one after another in one of the rich neighborhoods. She wanted enough for transport money and maybe they'd let her bring something sweet for Oscar, let him eat a block of chocolate. And then she'd need money to pay someone to sit with Lékè—Oscar had forbidden her from bringing the baby to the prison.

Elaine waited out the last day. The year had stormed through like one long winter.

She busied herself with Lékè to make the time pass quicker. After cleaning the house, she stayed in her room. She heard her landlady go out, come in, and out again. Elaine fussed over Lékè in a way she didn't normally indulge in. She tickled him underneath his neck. A wave of good feeling came over her. The lawyer would not give details but he sounded like things could be positive, that Oscar's innocence could be proven. Her techniques to make time go quickly worked. When the phone started ringing and Elaine checked the time, she was surprised that it was almost 10 pm.

"Hello. Who is this?"

"Hello. Can I speak to Elaine Marriot?" The man's voice on the other end was tinny. He was talking in a large space and his voice echoed against the walls.

"I'm Elaine. Who's this please?"

"Mustafah Jacobs. I'm a warden at the Joubert Prison."

"What is it?" Elaine asked but the question was futile.

"I'm sorry, ma'am."

To have known something and not known it at the same

time. To have been waiting for something and to have forgotten one was waiting. Mustafah Jacobs said many things
to console her that night. Elaine was in dire need of con-
solement—her husband was dead.

MONDAY 26TH OCTOBER 1992

Everything Oscar owned was put into a box. Elaine took
the bus as planned on Monday. She didn't stop to buy a
block of chocolate. The warden who'd phoned her the pre-
vious night met her in the administrative wing. Throughout
the gang battles that had been taking place in the prison,
he was the one to deliver the news to the grieving widows.
He handed the box with Oscar's name on it to Elaine with
a practiced heaviness. Inside the box was the photograph
Oscar had taken of her, his few clothes, and a wad of lined
paper with his handwriting—the letters. Elaine shivered as
she thought of her son. A wrist watch and pieces of paper
would not fill the gap of a father. She started to cry and the
warden shifted his feet. He looked down to the ground.

"I'm sorry, ma'am," he said, but her tears continued.

SATURDAY 24TH NOVEMBER 2012

Lékè opened his eyes and closed them again. He did
this repeatedly until he struggled to discern on which side
was the dream and which side reality. Everything was white
as though the atmosphere had transformed to moistened
particles of chalk dust. He looked around, noting that he
was in his studio. But he couldn't remember how he'd got
back there. A soft rapping got him to his feet.

Initially, when he opened the garage door, he could not
see anything but the fluffy fog-filled day.

"Who's there?" he called out and she emerged from
the softness.

"I woke you up." She sounded disappointed.

Lékè tried to hide his happiness to see her.

"I better go, it was a bad idea anyway."

"No, no, come in." He stepped aside to let her pass,
bending to close the door. When he turned around, she

was sitting on the edge of the bed, looking around.

"This is different, bunking down with a car for a room-mate," she said and Lékè smiled, relieved by her honesty.

"I wasn't expecting visitors."

She shrugged.

"How are you? How's your grandmother?" He was sorry he'd asked. He sat down, waiting for her to lift her head from her hands and her shoulders to stop shaking.

"I've had to use the permanent Frail Care. I can't take care of her anymore. They're good people but they don't understand her like I do, they don't know all the little things. They rang in the middle of the night because she was up-set and demanding to speak to me—disrupting the whole place. She knew who I was, though. Even just for one min-ute, she remembered my name."

Later they went for a walk outside in the fog and held hands. Lékè felt in a dream. He knew with a forceful cer-tainty that with his very next step, he would turn to wind and lift off.

WEDNESDAY 28TH NOVEMBER 2012

Marcus placed the phone down on the receiver. They'd confirmed his most recent fear. He hated doctors. Hated them. Ever since they had diagnosed Jane's sickness, he'd felt that way. Doctors lied. Instead of saying, "You're dy-ing," they say, "What's important going forward is quality of life." They say, "You may want to rearrange things, your daily schedule, to accommodate taking care of her."

"Baloney!" Marcus said out loud and snorted at his mental ranting.

He opened the drinks cupboard. He shouldn't have had the third glass of whiskey but since he did, he may as well proceed to the fourth.

If doctors had ever experienced somebody close to them dying, they would know that with that kind of situation comes a strange condition of denial, a certain "deafness."

Marcus took a swig from his glass, enjoying how plastic his thoughts had become. Like plasticine. Surely, if doctors understood about this condition of deafness, they would know to shout, to speak loud and direct into the ear of the person you needed to get the message across to: live each fucking day, love this person because they won't be here for much longer.

The doctor had wanted to know if he had anyone that would care for him as his condition worsened.

Should he call Lékè? Marcus toyed with the idea but watched it recede into the background. He went to place the empty glass in the kitchen sink, fixing his mind on bed. His cellphone rang so infrequently, it took him a few seconds to realize what the noise was.

"Hello." It took all his might to fight the drawl in his words.

"Marcus."

"Lékè! How're you? You there?"

"I wanted to just…"

"Yes, how are you doing?"

"I'm fine. I'm OK."

"Good good. How's Red? Everything OK?"

"It's fine, Marcus. I was checking in."

"Oh!" Marcus sat down at the kitchen table.

"How are you?" Lékè asked.

"I'm all right. I was at the…I'm all right, a bit bored really. The University is about to close. After graduation. I think I'll just retire next year."

"You already are."

"But I mean just leave properly. They let me stay on all these years but…I think I'll leave properly now."

Lékè didn't know what to say.

"Well. So thanks for the call, son. Did you read the things I gave to you?"

"Yes."

"Ah."

"I also wanted to tell you something."

"Yes? You there, Lékè?"

A silence peaked.

"Lékè?"

"See you on Sunday, Marcus."

"Great, son. Yes, see you Sunday."

SATURDAY 1ST DECEMBER 2012

"Can you help me?" Lékè asked, looking across at the Babaláwo. The skin on the man's face reminded Lékè of his leather brogues. The eyes were bloodshot.

They were sitting at a table, but when Lékè looked down, he realized they were floating. The ground was somewhere far below and this fact did not bother him.

The Babaláwo leaned forward and studied Lékè. "You still have your baby eyes," he said. "People don't understand like us Babaláwos do, just as babies lose their milk teeth, they lose their baby eyes too. Followers cannot tell the difference but we can."

As the Babaláwo spoke, Lékè kept looking down. The ground was getting closer.

"Same way you need adult teeth as you grow into the world, you need a new pair of eyes to really be able to focus. The baby is from the spirit world with spirit eyes. That makes for an unsettled life, when the child keeps her baby eyes."

"So you can't help me then?"

"Your life is full of illusions. Things seen that aren't there, things that are there remaining unseen."

"But what about the curse though? That's why I'm here."

The Babaláwo shook his head.

"What? Can't you remove it?"

"It's impossible."

"But you're him, right? It was your curse, you were the one my great-grandparents came to?"

He nodded.

"So then? Do something. By any means, please." The table was rising again and the ground moved further away. "I love her, you see?"

"OK, give me a piece of your heart." The Babaláwo pointed at Lékè's breast pocket.

Lékè reached into his pocket and pulled out his photograph. He now knew what "E" stood for—Elaine.

"I'll take this," the Babaláwo said, "as an offering up of yourself. A token."

"So, you can reverse it?"

"There is one possibility. Take." The Babaláwo placed two tokens, a cowry shell and a piece of bone into Lékè's cupped hands. "Place one in each hand, don't let me see which." He spread the cowhide on the table and sprinkled some sand on it for notation. He gathered the sixteen palm-nuts into his left hand and then exchanged. Two left. He made a mark in the sand.

The Babaláwo continued throwing until he had a full reading.

"Well?" Lékè asked.

"Show me what's in your left hand."

The cowry shell. "What does that mean?" Lékè asked "Can you remove the curse?"

"Yes. On one condition."

"What's that?

The Babaláwo gathered up the cowries and repeated the ritual, consulting Ifa. When he'd finished, he shook his head.

"What's wrong?"'

"Show me your left hand."

The bone.

"There will be difficulty," the Babaláwo said.

"What do you mean? What's the condition?"

"That's the condition."

The young man looked confused.

"Ifa will undo the curse. There is no sacrifice required except to propitiate Èṣù with the entrails of a guinea fowl and its breast feathers intact."

"Is that all?"

"Well, as I said there is a condition. And the condition is there is a condition but you'll never know what it is. There is a condition though and it will come and when it comes, you'll know this is it but you don't know what you're wait-ing for and you don't know when it's coming. That's the condition."

"A life of dread?" Lékè asked, in the dream.

"No." The Babaláwo shook his head. "Just a life."

Lékè looked down as the ground drew closer and closer until, finally, he could feel the warm earth beneath his bare feet.

The Babaláwo dissolved. Lékè stood from the table and walked away, his feet tapping the ground. Tap. Tap.

◈◈

Lékè woke to the rain tapping his tin roof. Tap. Tap. The sting of ammonia was still in the air from his last cleaning session despite the window he'd left open for ventilation. He worried water would come in through the open window and wondered when summer would settle in properly.

He banged his hand onto the space beside him on the mattress, hoping to collide with a soft body. Nothing.

He was almost certain he was alone. He lay still, remembering his dream and wondering whether to get up and check if the photograph of Elaine was still in its place, when he heard the click of his fridge door opening and the refrigerator light showing Tsotso in white flannel pajamas.

"I'm hungry." Her flat tone. "And your cupboards are bare."

WEDNESDAY 19TH FEBRUARY 2013

"How much will it cost?" Tsotso asked.

"Four hundred," Lékè replied.

"Rands?"

He shot her a look.

"That's a chunk of cash, Lékè."

The robot turned green and Lékè pulled off. "Marcus has given me the money."

"I thought you said he doesn't believe in such things?"

"He changed his mind. He said I should do whatever I need to."

"OK, so you're freaking me out. I mean, are you serious? A sangoma?"

"Not just anyone, Marcus tracked down one he

trusts. The woman who used to care for me gave the recommendation."

"Your nanny's sangoma?"

Lékè kept his eyes on the road. "You don't have to come with me but I'm asking you to. I'll do it either way."

"You know I'll come so don't be like that." She sucked her teeth and Lékè tried to hide his smile.

They drove on in silence, pulling up at the last flat they'd circled in the "Cape Ads." The rent was good. It was near the Frail Care and it was on the ground floor.

Tsotso didn't want the trauma of moving the piano up flights of stairs.

Lékè moved to open his car door and Tsotso touched his back.

"I don't want this hanging over our heads. I'll go with you but promise me that will be it."

"I promise."

The Saturday morning traffic into Gugulethu had been heavy. Something was happening at the civic hall, a gathering of some sort. Large banners waved in the breeze and the stamp of toi-toing struck a beat through the air. They parked Red alongside a spaza shop. A dog trailed them as they walked past a large sign, "Yellow Door Nightclub." They entered the compound next door. The sangoma, Sis' Lerato, was an herbalist as well as a part-time Xhosa teacher.

"Good morning," Lékè said when she opened the door, Tsotso standing behind him.

Sis' Lerato, heavy-set, her feet in plastic slippers, looked ordinary.

"Lightness would never recognize you now," she said, opening the door wide so they walked past her into a large living area. "Go straight through, to the back. I'll be with you in a bit."

When she returned, she was wearing a string of beads that covered her face. Lékè and Tsotso sat, cross-legged on one end of a long mat, and she now joined them, sitting on the opposite end. Different sized jars, a few empty, others too dark to tell the contents, and still others with some animal offal floating in transparent liquid, lined one of the walls of the room. A stash of old newspapers in a corner and small grease-proof paper wrapped parcels, each the size of a banana, were arranged on top of a sturdy wooden shelf. The curtains were drawn but the bright day's light filtered through the thin red fabric, giving everything a faintly red tinge.

"Welcome." Sis' Lerato settled herself, her voice hushed. "Yes. Yes. Welcome." She pointed to the white candlestick they'd been asked to bring, and a box of matches. She lit the candle. "Welcome. Welcome, Lékè. Welcome to our daughter, Tsotso."

As she spoke, the beads clicked against each other, a twittering kind of rain. Lékè listened. He wasn't sure what he was listening for but he listened. She was rattling off a series of names that he didn't recognize. Marcus had wasted his money.

"One of our children wants to make herbs and heal."

"What does that mean?" Lékè asked, speaking for the first time since the consultation started.

"Your ancestors are speaking. They say they want a life, a child. One of them will return to practice my work—healing. It is a truce with the sangoma-curse that hovers over your life. The child devotes its life to the practice of divination and the curse will cease."

"I don't understand, though, I don't have any children."

Sis' Lerato looked beyond Lékè, to Tsotso who met her eyes and then averted her gaze. "You will understand soon."

Sis' Lerato collected a stash of dried wild sage and lit it. Soon a heavy smoke filled the small room. The pungent smell would stay with Lékè for several weeks afterwards.

Lékè didn't understand much of what the ancestors said. Through Sis' Lerato they spoke of farms, crops that weren't rotated when they should have been, land that had to be reclaimed. Each time a different ancestor spoke, Sis' Lerato would wriggle in her body and seemed to take on the persona of whoever was speaking. A high-pitched voice demanded Lékè make weekly donations, for six months, to the closest shelter.

"What?" Lékè was confused.

Sis' Lerato turned her head like an aerial picking signal. Then, in the high-pitched voice again, "You need to give back, Lékè. Give back what was taken."

A different voice, deep, wanted Lékè to buy a motorbike but also warned against drinking and driving. It seemed a joke and Sis' Lerato laughed, loud guffaws. Sometimes she lapsed into a language that neither Tsotso nor Lékè recognized. It felt as though the conversation was really between her and the ancestors; Lékè and Tsotso were merely there to watch.

"You OK?" Tsotso asked, noticing Lékè had started fidgeting.

"My skin's itching." A steady fire grew along his skin, moving over the surface of his body like a bee swarm. It wasn't painful. Uncomfortable, yes. Despite this, Lékè stayed sitting, scratching his body as the bee swarm moved from his shoulder to his back to underneath his bare feet. "Yes," Sis' Lerato kept on saying. "Yes, Lékè. Yes. Bom Boy. You are back now. You are finally here." After twenty minutes, the itching abated, the bee swarm flew away. Lékè relaxed his body, relieved but exhausted.

After they paid her and were already standing at the threshold, she took Lékè's hand. "You have a lot of ancestors. A lot of your people are on the other side."

Lékè looked at her. He was shaken, unsure of what had just taken place. She had called him Bom Boy, he was sure of that.

"Your mother," she said as they reached the door. "I mean your birth mother. She wasn't there." She let go of his hand. "Your mother was not there."

Lékè drove out of Gugulethu, pulling to the left of the road as cars overtook him. He balanced the wheel with one hand, held Tsotso's hand with the other. The car windows were down and a warm wind, distinctly summer, brushed his face.

"What did she mean 'give back?'" Tsotso asked as they joined the N2.

Lékè used both hands to maneuver. "I should have told you before. I'm a thief. In the past, I've taken things that didn't belong to me. I'm not going to justify it. I was wrong."

Tsotso was silent for a while. "Are you going to do it?"

"Do what?"

"Give back?"

"Yes."

"And your mother? You'll try and find her," Tsotso said.

Lékè changed gear, picking up speed. After all the cold and wet, he enjoyed the feel of the sun on his face.

Acknowledgments

To my family—thanks for all your love, support and friendship.

Thank you to Joanne Hichens. You managed to bring a combination of commitment, compassion and straight-edged feedback and I appreciate all that I have learnt through your guidance.

Thank you to Colleen Higgs of Modjaji Books and Jessica Powers of Catalyst Press—for saying "yes."

To my wonderful motley crew of friends: thanks for not disowning me because instead of coming out with you, I went home to write.

Thanks Kira, Rebecca, and Hayley for reading and commenting.

Over the course of writing this story I spoke to and sourced information from a wide group of people: doctors, friends, dog-breeders, nurses, ex-prisoners, prison workers, sangomas, lawyers (it's a very long list)—thank you all for generously explaining everything I asked you to and doing it with grace. Thanks to Heather Parker Lewis for the information you supplied me with on prisons and prison-life.

Mandy and James Campbell-Miller and Tony Dallas, thanks for letting me write in your homes.

❧❧